About the Author

Aubrey is an Atlanta-based author. He spent nearly a decade working in the field of microbiology and research. He is an avid book collector, a passion he shares with his wife. He uses his love of science and storytelling to create fun, thought-provoking stories. When he isn't writing, he usually has his head buried in a book or is out creating memories with his family.

Micro Dad Fights a Cold

Aubrey Williams

Micro Dad Fights a Cold

Olympia Publishers
London

www.olympiapublishers.com
OLYMPIA PAPERBACK EDITION

A CIP catalogue record for this title is
available from the British Library.

ISBN: 978-1-80439-077-1

This is a work of fiction.
Names, characters, places and incidents originate from the writer's
imagination. Any resemblance to actual persons, living or dead, is
purely coincidental.

First Published in 2023

Olympia Publishers
Tallis House
2 Tallis Street
London
EC4Y 0AB

Printed in Great Britain

Dedication

I dedicate this book to the dreamers.

Acknowledgements

Thank you to my wife, Cynthia, for your endless support and encouragement as I took the leap of faith to write this book, and to my kids, Derrick and Maya, thank you for inspiring me to always strive to achieve more.

Prologue

"Shhhh! No talking and eyes on your open paper. I mean you, Mr. Stevens," Mrs. Bryant said as she sat at her desk and stared across the classroom like a hawk.

Her sixth-grade class sat silently as they took their science tests. It was the first one of the year, so each student was determined to get a good grade. Pairs of eyes gazed down at the stapled packet of papers in front of them. They read every question closely then drew uneven circles around answers A, B, C or D. Some circled answer after answer quickly while others had to stop and think for a few seconds at a time.

But not everyone was able to focus on the test. Eddie Moore, also known as "Sneezing Eddie", was a tall, husky kid with dark hair and a large personality, who was often mistaken for an eighth grader even before he started middle school. He sat in his chair with his head tilted backward and his eyes glued to the ceiling. His nose was running again for the fifth time, so he had to lean back to stop it from dripping all over his desk. School had only started a few weeks before, but Eddie had already been sick with a cold twice. He wanted to win the perfect attendance award at the end of the year like he had done every year throughout elementary school, so he was never willing to miss a day.

Once, he sneezed ten times in a row while the teacher was in front of the classroom. Everyone, including the teacher, laughed wildly. That's how he earned the name "Sneezing Eddie". He wasn't too happy about the nickname, especially since he was in middle school now, and he knew that nicknames could last forever.

As his nose leaked, Eddie reached into his jacket pocket and pulled out a used piece of tissue and cleaned his runny nose. Just before putting the paper back in his pocket, Eddie glanced at it and noticed it was soggy and full of holes. The sight of the wet, used-up paper made him uneasy, so he raised his hand.

"Mrs. Bryant, can I go to the trashcan, please?"

"Yes, Sn—, I mean, Eddie," she said thoughtfully then continued glaring at the rest of the class.

Eddie stood up to walk to the trashcan which sat across the room, but he only made it a few steps before the tip of his nose began to tickle. Time slowed to a crawl as Eddie attempted to walk past his classmates' desks, trying as hard as he could to hold back another sneeze. He tilted his head backward again and took a deep breath, filling his lungs with air. He thought the moment had passed, but his head began to fall forward, preparing to spray air and tiny droplets of spit all over the other students.

He lifted his hand to block the sneeze, but he only had less than a second to cover his mouth and nose. It was a race against time. His hand was barely an inch away from his face when he roared "achoo" and sprayed a cloud of mist toward the students in the third row.

Everyone jumped and immediately took cover, using their tests as shields. Only one student named Alex, who sat a few rows behind Eddie, lifted his head and became a direct target for the shower of spit. There was no escaping it. The spray flew right at him. All he could do was stare like a deer stunned by headlights as he was showered.

Sneezing Eddie quickly gave a guilty smile.

"Sorry," he said awkwardly then lumbered over to the trashcan to throw away the used tissue before returning to his seat and finishing his test.

Chapter 1

It was a Thursday morning. Autumn had just begun, so the air had a slight chill. The leaves high up in the trees were beginning to change from green to a mixture of different stages of rust and had not yet begun to fall. It was almost the perfect day.

Frank and Camille hustled through their daily morning routines. Frank stood by the stove and whipped up another batch of pancakes while Camille sat at the kitchen table and pleaded with their energetic and stubborn four-year-old daughter, Maya, to finish her breakfast. Camille had been late getting Maya to pre-school all week, and it seemed as though a fourth day of being tardy was looming, despite Camille's efforts to stop Maya from using her fork and knife as flying saucers in a never-ending game she liked to call "Space Invaders". Camille, normally calm and carefree, was reaching her breaking point.

As Camille's impatience grew, twelve-year-old Alex strolled down the stairs and into the kitchen. He was still wearing his robe, and his long, dark, curly hair was messy and in need of a comb. He looked exhausted. His eyes were tired and bloodshot. His caramel-colored skin looked clammy and damp, as if he had just finished running a race. When he reached his parents, he spoke in a whisper.

"I'm not feeling very good," he said between coughs. "My throat really hurts."

"Oh no, honey. You look awful," said Camille, rushing to him.

"Oh, he's just faking because he has a math test today," Frank said with a grin while flipping another one of his golden-brown pancakes.

Alex shot his dad an intense look from across the room. Everyone in the family knew just how much Alex loved math, so there was no way he would ever purposely miss a test.

"Seriously, Frank, he looks pretty sick. Come take a look at him, doctor," said Camille.

Frank slid the last of the pancakes onto a plate, removed his "Kiss the Cook" apron, and walked over to Alex.

"Let's take a look at you, Al," he said then gently touched Alex's neck directly underneath his chin. Suddenly, as if by magic, Frank's medical kit appeared in the blink of an eye.

"We've been married for twelve years, and I still don't know how you do that," Camille said.

"You know, sometimes healing just—"

"Takes a little magic," Camille interrupted. "I at least know your catchphrase after all these years." Then she gave Frank a peck on the cheek and flashed a light smile.

"Gross," Alex said with a look of complete disgust. "I thought I was sick before, but you guys are making me feel even worse."

"Don't be a hater, Al," Frank said and continued his checkup.

He removed a silver object from his blue-and-white medical kit then moved to the side of Alex's head. The black plastic cone-shaped tip of the otoscope plunged into Alex's ears as the device shone light into each dark opening. Next, Frank used a wooden tongue depressor, that was identical to a popsicle stick, and a flashlight to examine his throat. Frank's forehead wrinkled a few times and his eyes narrowed slightly as he gazed into his mouth. Alex instantly recognized the look. It was the look Frank always made when he knew he had to give bad news.

Frank reached into the bag again and took out a stethoscope. He pressed it to Alex's chest and back. Alex shivered every time the round metal head of the device touched his bare skin. Frank listened closely to Alex's lungs and heart with the tool. Afterwards, he used a thermometer to check Alex's temperature. Alex stood with his arms crossed as he held the slim object under his tongue and waited for it to beep loudly.

Seconds later, Frank removed it from Alex's mouth then stared at the numbers displayed on the small screen.

"You don't have a fever or swollen lymph nodes, but because of your cough, sore throat, and runny nose, I'd say you have a pretty bad cold."

"Looks like you're staying home today, sweetie," said Camille. "Frank, I have a meeting with our new clients. Can you stay home with him?"

"Sure. I'll ask Dr. Patel to look after my patients today. You get to hang with me today, Al," Frank said with a heartfelt smile aimed at Alex.

Alex immediately interjected. "Whoa, I actually feel better already!" he managed to shout, despite his rough, raspy voice. "No one has to stay home with me because I can go to school. I feel fine. Don't worry," he said with a dismissive wave of the hand.

"You can't go to school if you're sick, Alex," said Frank.

"Listen to your dad, sweetie. Besides, Mrs. Green will let you retake your math test when you get back," said Camille, resting a hand on Alex's shoulder.

"It's not that," Alex said softly. "The science fair's today, and I'm sure I can win with my invention. I've been working on it every night for weeks. Zoey Perez has been saying that she's definitely going to win, but I know I can finally beat her."

"Why didn't you tell us about the science fair, Al?" Frank asked.

"I wanted to surprise you when I came home with the trophy after school," Alex said with a sniffle then gave his mom a quick glance before turning back to Frank, "and I used a few parts from Mom's hair dryer. I didn't think she'd be too mad once she found out it was sacrificed for a good cause."

"That's why I couldn't dry my hair last week? I went to work looking like I had been caught in a rainstorm," Camille said, "but I guess I don't mind donating my hair dryer and a few good hair days to your project. What is it, anyway?"

"I made a remote-control car," Alex mumbled while staring down at the floor. "I found spare parts wherever I could. It's powered by a secret ingredient for a battery."

"That sounds awesome, Al. I'm sure it would be tough for Zoey to beat, but you can't go to school while you're sick. You're contagious and could get all your friends and classmates sick, too. There will be other science fairs," Frank said grimly as he walked over to him and placed a small cup filled with a crimson-colored medicine into his hand.

"Good thinking, Dad," Alex said as he brought the cup up to his lips. "I'll take the medicine then go to school."

"That medicine's to help you sleep, Al," Frank said.

Alex stopped just before taking a sip then brought the cup down to his side. "But Dad, please. Isn't there something you can do to help me get better so I can go to school? You're a doctor. Fix me," Alex started to beg.

"Alex, your dad can't work magic. He's just a doctor. Rest and medicine will help you get better. Now, go upstairs and get back in bed."

"But Mom!" Alex tried to continue but was quickly silenced.

"Sorry, Alex. Back to bed. I have to take your sister to school, and we're already running late. Take your medicine, sweetie, then get right back in bed. I'll check on you boys later," Camille said firmly.

Without another word, Alex turned and stomped up the steps. His slippers glided across the wooden floor in the hallway then his bedroom door slammed shut. Camille frowned as she grabbed her "My Kids Don't Need Google, They Have Their Mom" coffee mug. She gave Frank a quick kiss then followed Maya out the door, leaving Frank alone with a stack of pancakes and a pile of dirty dishes to clean.

Chapter 2

Alex sat alone in his room deciding how he could make his escape and get to school without his dad noticing his absence. The cup of medicine sat on his nightstand. He had spent far too many nights working on his project to just give up, stay in bed and sleep just because he was sick. He was determined to win the first-place trophy in the science fair no matter what, but winning the trophy wasn't his only motivation. He was driven by the need to defeat his archenemy more than anything else.

Alex had met Zoey Perez the first day of kindergarten. She had introduced herself by loudly criticizing Alex's less than remarkable drawing. She shouted that hers was much better than his then proceeded to draw a large, blue castle over his small, green cow. She had pestered him ever since.

With Zoey, he was always second place. If she did slightly better than him on a test, she would never miss the opportunity to rub it in his face. If Alex did one less jumping jack than her in gym class, Zoey would be sure to make him aware. Their rivalry had no limits.

What made matters worse, Zoey had been in every single one of Alex's classes for five years in a row. It was complete torture. There was no escape from her and her constant criticism. The only thing that comforted Alex was the fact that elementary school had to end. He imagined he would go off to bigger and better things in middle school and would no longer have to see Zoey's mocking smile or hear her say, "Well, it looks like I beat you again, Alex." He just knew he would be rid of her forever once elementary school ended.

On his last day as a fifth grader, Alex's cheeks hurt from his constant smiling. He almost exploded with joy every time he thought about never being in another class with Zoey again, and when the bell rang to end the day, he celebrated his freedom from school and from her. He had an amazing, fun-filled summer, and to his parent's surprise, he talked endlessly about how excited he was to start the sixth grade.

Usually, as the start of the next school year came around the corner and the end of summer vacation got closer, Alex always complained about how short the break was and said that he planned to write a strongly worded letter to the President to extend summer break for at least another two months. It was his yearly joke but not this time. Going to the sixth grade was different. He counted the days until he could walk into middle school.

His first day, Alex woke up filled with energy and excitement as a smile stayed glued to his face. He ate breakfast with it. He rode the bus to school and walked to his first sixth-grade class with it. He didn't think anything could ruin his perfect day, but as he got closer to the doorway of the classroom, he heard the horrible sound of a familiar voice.

He was sure he was having a nightmare. He even pinched his right hand to make sure he wasn't asleep, but Alex quickly realized he was very much awake when Zoey turned to the door, flashed a beaming smile of her own then shouted, "Hi, Alex! I'm so happy to see you!"

To make matters worse, he was assigned a seat right next to her, because their teacher, Mr. Finn, said that they looked like such good friends. She spent the next ten minutes telling him about how great her summer had been and how excited she was to have another class with him. The last part she said with a cartoonishly huge grin, showing every bit of her rainbow-colored braces. Alex's big, beaming smile had faded long before as he sat there without saying a word.

Fortunately for him, Zoey wasn't in every one of his classes. She was only in four out of six, but she did continue sitting beside him in each one. In science class, their last class of the day, their teacher, Mrs. Bryant, announced there would be a science fair in just a few weeks for every sixth grader who wanted to participate. She urged them all to start thinking of exciting inventions to create.

Alex was thrilled when he heard the news. Besides math, he loved science and couldn't think of anything more fun than inventing something amazing. Zoey seemed to read his mind or just noticed the large smile that suddenly appeared on his face, because she instantly looked over at him and whispered, "I'm going to make something for the science fair. It would be so cool if you invented something, too. I think you'd do great. Good luck."

Alex couldn't help but smile at Zoey's friendliness. "Maybe she changed this summer," he thought. "Maybe she isn't so bad after all."

Just as he was going to thank her and wish her luck too, Zoey leaned over again and whispered casually, "You're going to need all the luck you can get if you think you're going to beat me, Alex." Then she flashed him another bright, metallic smile.

Alex almost erupted but managed to keep his cool. From that moment on he had one goal, and it was to win first place in the science fair. It was his chance to outshine Zoey. He didn't just want to beat her. He wanted to beat her so badly that it would haunt her dreams forever. He wanted to make her invention look worse than she had made his green cow look in kindergarten. Alex knew that a first-place trophy would make up for every time she had ever celebrated his loss. He couldn't let anything stop him from getting to the science fair.

Back in his room, his first idea was to make a life-sized dummy of himself using pillows dressed in a pair of his pajamas and engineered with a pulley system to fool his dad. It would be just like the old movies he had seen on TV. But as Alex attempted to launch his master plan, he began to cough uncontrollably. He became light-headed and immediately had to lie down.

Even after several minutes of coughing and sniffling in bed, he wasn't discouraged. He thought of a new plan, and it was brilliant. He would shuffle to his dad, look him straight in the eyes and say, "Please let me go to school!" Then he would beg and not just any begging. He would do the ultimate begging. He would perform the best begging routine of his life. He wanted to be nominated for an award for the begging he planned to do. He would plead his case and his dad would have to say yes. That was the entire plan. It wasn't ideal, but Alex left his pride next to his incomplete pillow-dummy.

He picked himself up out of bed and made his way into the hallway. He walked unsteadily as his body became more and more exhausted and his eyes grew increasingly harder to keep open. After a moment, he rested his head on the hallway wall, feeling the powerful urge to sleep. Suddenly, he heard a sound coming from his dad's office. It wasn't very loud, but Alex had never heard anything like it coming from the room before. It was like metal gears gliding past one another.

Suddenly filled with a bit more energy, Alex crept over to the office and opened the door carefully without making a sound.

He peeked his head inside and began scanning the room, but nothing was out of the ordinary. In fact, everything was normal. It wasn't until Alex's eyes landed on his dad's bookcase that he began to feel uneasy.

The large oak bookcase was as it always was, perfectly neat and tidy, the way Frank always kept it. Rows of books spread across each of its shelves, but the bookcase itself wasn't in its usual place beside a large map of the world that covered the entire wall. It was somehow standing several feet to the left, which was odd given how heavy and unmovable it appeared to be.

After staring in disbelief for a moment, Alex shifted his gaze to the right where a figure stood in front of a large square hole in the wall where the bookcase once was. Terror quickly gripped him, and his heart began to pound uncontrollably. The figure was tall and muscular. It wore a blue-and-white suit, reminding Alex of an afternoon sky. The suit was made of thin armor that fit its body perfectly. A silver belt with too many pockets to count was wrapped tightly around its waist.

Behind the mysterious person, within the secret opening, Alex could see objects resting on metal hooks. He couldn't tell what most of the items were except for one. It was a miniature blue-and-white airplane that was as small as a child's toy. The figure, completely unaware of Alex's presence, continued to face the secret room. Then it placed its hands on its hips with its elbows bent. The power pose made it look like it had just fallen out of a comic book.

Alex's heart continued to race. He was beyond terrified. A strange person was standing in his dad's office wearing a weird costume. He didn't know whether to yell for help or run away, so he just stood frozen in place.

After a few seconds of watching the man stand there with his armored hands on his hips, as if he were waiting for a round of applause, Alex slowly began to relax. His pulse began to slow, and his look of terror turned into amazement. The man didn't seem frightening at all. His silly behavior actually seemed a bit familiar.

Alex's curiosity finally got the better of him, and moments later he let out a sudden, "Hi."

The man quickly turned to Alex, his face barely visible behind a thin screen attached to an armored helmet.

Suddenly, a high-pitched squeal spilled out of the man. "Ahh!" he said just before vanishing in a flash of light.

Alex's jaw dropped. Every inch of his body became numb. He was completely shocked. Being sick and the unexpected disappearance of a masked man in his dad's office quickly took their toll and left him feeling overwhelmed and dizzy. The room started to spin.

Alex felt like he was on a rollercoaster doing loop after loop. His eyelids became as heavy as bricks. He started to sway back and forth until he could no longer keep himself standing. A moment later, his legs became lifeless, and he fell to the floor.

Chapter 3

Alex woke up in bed. He could barely open his eyes, but he could feel the familiar warmth and softness of the pillows and mattress that gave him comfort every night. He didn't know how he had made it back to his room, but the last moments before he fainted slowly began to resurface in his mind, and confusion quickly followed. Suddenly, he heard a voice near him.

"Alex, are you okay?" said Frank from somewhere in the room.

Alex became overjoyed at the sound of his dad's voice.

"That all must have been a dream," he thought.

"Being sick must be giving me nightmares," Alex said aloud. "Dad, I guess I'm sicker than I thought. I had a dream that some guy in a costume was standing in your office, then he disappeared when he saw me."

"It's not a costume," Frank mumbled, barely loud enough for Alex to hear. "And I happen to think it's a pretty cool suit."

Thinking his cold was still playing tricks on him, Alex ignored his dad's comment and began stretching to relieve the aches in his neck and back. Finally feeling satisfied, he quickly remembered his plan to beg his dad to let him go to school.

"I think I'm feeling better, Dad," he lied and began searching his bedroom to find Frank and start the begging process. He looked left and right but saw nothing but his bedroom furniture and posters of LeBron James and Steph Curry taped to the walls.

Without warning, Frank stepped away from the farthest

corner of the room, out of the shadows, and into the gleaming sunlight. The armored suit he wore glistened as the light struck it, making him shine brighter than a star in a cloudless night sky.

Alex was amazed. He had only ever seen his dad dressed in nice suits and lab coats, except for one Halloween when everyone in the family dressed like a different superhero character. Frank had simply donned a thin cloth mask and a short cape made from a beach towel.

"Dad, it was you in the office?" Alex stammered. "Are you going to Comic Con or somethin'?"

Frank was instantly deflated by the comment. "I finally reveal my secret identity to you, and you think that I'm wearing this to go to a comic book convention? Seriously?" Frank groaned.

"Secret identity? I didn't know you had a secret identity. Does Mom know?" Alex asked with growing enthusiasm.

"No, Mom doesn't know. The key word in that sentence was secret, Al," Frank said with a gentle smile then sat on the bed next to Alex.

"Why does it have to be a secret? Do you wear that costume around the house when no one is home or when we're all asleep, like a role play game?"

"What? No," said Frank. "Well, actually, it's kind of hard to explain."

Alex had a million questions in his head, but his dad seemed unwilling to answer them, which was strange to Alex, because they had always talked about everything. There were never any secrets between them. Every day, no matter if it was good or bad, they told each other about it. In fact, every night during dinner, each family member got a chance to talk about how his or her day had been, even Maya, who usually spent most of her talk-time complaining about some preschooler refusing to share a toy or cutting her in line to go down the slide during recess.

Silence filled the room. Frank sat as still as a statue and stared blankly at Alex, with his mouth slightly open as if he wanted to form sentences but couldn't quite remember how. Alex stared back at his dad with curiosity as his eyes left his dad's confused face and became fixed on the image in the center of the glimmering suit. The design was hypnotizing and seemed to draw Alex into it. Carved into the armor were two medical instruments easily recognizable by everyone worldwide, a large stethoscope and a thermometer, but they were arranged oddly on the thin metal suit.

The stethoscope was entangled around the thermometer like a snake wrapped around its prey. The two earbuds were positioned on both sides of the thermometer, and the stethoscope's long tubing twisted around the device until the circular end of its long tail came to a stop on the left side of Frank's chest, directly above where his heart would be. Alex knew the two items symbolized health and medicine but didn't understand why his dad had them engraved in the middle of a costume he had known nothing about. Only people in comic books or on television wore clothes with symbols in the middle of them.

Suddenly, a lightbulb went off in Alex's mind. His large round eyes grew even wider as everything quickly became very clear to him.

"You're a superhero!" he exclaimed then began coughing intensely.

"You have to take it easy, Alex," Frank said, patting him on the back lightly. "You're still sick and you can hurt your throat even more by yelling so much."

"But Dad, this is amazing. How did you disappear? Is that your superpower? Can you fly in that suit? Why don't you have a cape? Do you have a secret lair underneath the house like the Batcave?" The questions came pouring out of Alex's mouth as he sniffled and found it increasingly more difficult to breathe from his congested nose and talk at the same time.

"Slow down, Alex. Slow down. I'm not a superhero," Frank said calmly, using his fingers to quote "superhero". "I made this suit a long time ago to fight diseases. I've fought some pretty tough viruses and bacteria that have made you guys sick over the years. That's all."

Confusion swept through Alex. "But you always took care of us when we were sick by giving us medicine and making us soup," he said as he remembered the dozens of times his dad had sat with him and watched television while he ate delicious homemade chicken noodle soup. "How else were you fighting the diseases?"

"You're right, Al," Frank responded. "I do always make you soup and give you medicine, but the medicine usually just made you sleep. Don't you remember always feeling better when you woke up?"

Alex immediately searched his mind for memories of being sick. He remembered talking to his dad or watching a television show during many instances. His eyelids would become heavy, then he would slowly drift off to sleep. Every time he woke up, he always felt better, as if he had only been sick in a dream. He constantly had the feeling of not being completely sure he had ever been sick at all.

On one occasion just a few years before, Camille had become sick with the flu right before the family was scheduled to take a trip to the beach. Alex had woken up that day full of excitement, but his enthusiasm soon disappeared with one look at his mom. She looked terrible. Her skin was pale, she coughed like she was choking on bees, and she couldn't move an inch out of bed.

She was typically fun and carefree, making her easy to talk to and to love. But when she was sick, she was miserable, cranky, and completely helpless. It was difficult for Alex to watch. He was sure the trip would be cancelled, but his dad assured him that his mom just had "a little bug" and would feel better in no time. Frank promised they would all still go to the beach once Alex got home from school.

Alex was skeptical, of course. He knew that Camille couldn't even get out of bed, much less take a trip in just a few short hours, but after school, Alex got off the bus and slowly walked into the house, expecting to hear the bad news from his dad. Surprisingly, Camille was the one who greeted him when he walked in. She sat at the kitchen table, drinking a hot cup of tea then smiled brightly when she saw him. Her big, brown eyes lit up. Her skin, the color of honey, glowed beautifully, and her warmth filled the room.

Alex was shocked when he saw her. He stared at her blankly and had to force himself to speak. She probably should have gone to the hospital just a few hours earlier, but now she looked as if she could run a marathon. She was completely healthy, as if she had never been sick at all.

The entire family went to the beach that day. Alex thought about his mom's unbelievable recovery for weeks, but eventually, the memory faded, and all he could remember was the fun he had had on the trip.

As the memories resurfaced, they began taking shape in Alex's mind. He knew it was strange that his family never stayed sick for long and always achieved some amazing recovery, but he could never quite understand why. He thought about many other instances until the sound of Frank's voice brought him back to the present moment.

"This might sound crazy," Frank continued, "but when I wear this suit, I can shrink to extremely small sizes, so small that you couldn't see me if I were standing on the tip of your nose. Once I'm that small, I fight the diseases that make you sick from the inside." He quickly offered Alex a painfully awkward smile.

Alex no longer looked amazed. Frank's announcement hit him hard like a high-speed train. He looked as if his brain had short-circuited and all his thoughts had stopped. Frank noticed the blank expression and attempted to trigger a response.

"Pretty weird, huh?" he muttered.

"Yeah, pretty weird," Alex agreed after staying silent for a few seconds, "but so cool!" he howled with excitement and restarted his line of questioning.

"What do our insides look like? Does it smell? How do you get in and out?"

"Well, I'm glad you're not totally freaked out right now," Frank said with a laugh.

Alex fired off question after question before suddenly becoming serious. "Were you planning on helping me today so that I could go to the science fair?" he asked.

Frank flashed a warm smile at him and shrugged. "I saw how important it was to you, so I wanted to help."

Alex bit the inside of his lip gently then gazed down at his bed. For weeks, he couldn't wait until the day of the science fair, but when he woke up that morning with a cold, there was something deep inside of him that was glad. If he was forced to stay home because he was sick, then he wouldn't have to face

Zoey in yet another competition and lose.

"Thanks, Dad. But I think it's too late. The science fair starts in a few hours. I don't think I'll feel better in time," he said glumly. "My throat is still really sore, I can't breathe from my nose, and I cough every ten seconds. Besides, I probably wouldn't win anyway. Zoey always beats me. I don't know why I even try."

Frank placed a hand on Alex's shoulder. "You were so excited this morning when you told us about your invention. You said you worked hard on it every night for weeks, right? It doesn't matter if you win or lose, but you deserve the chance to show what you've created, compete, and have fun, Al. Your mom was right, I can't do magic, but I can try my best to help you get to the science fair, feel great, and not spread this virus while you're there. What do you say?"

After a moment of silence, Alex lifted his head and smiled. "Let's do it."

Chapter 4

"What do I need to do?" asked Alex.

"Nothing much," Frank replied as he got to his feet and walked to the middle of the room. "Just sit here and relax. You really should be resting."

"Wait, c'mon. I can't help? I thought I was like your sidekick now that I know you're a superhero, Dad," Alex responded with a tense, irritated expression.

"You're helping more than you know, Alex. Your white blood cells work extremely hard fighting diseases, and you produce those cells, so you really are doing a lot. I'm just providing a little extra backup for them, is all."

"But can't I at least talk to you while you're working? That way I can give you status updates on how I'm feeling. How else would you really know if what you're doing is working? We can use my walkie-talkies!" Without an answer, Alex excitedly shuffled to his nightstand and took out two red walkies with short antennas that stuck out from the tops of them.

"Please, Dad. We're a team."

Frank looked at Alex with uncertainty. He had been on dozens of missions to help the family and all without them helping or even knowing anything about it, but this time was different now that Alex knew his secret identity. This time, they really could work as a team.

"I guess I could use a good command center." Frank finally gave in. "Let's get to work." Frank reached into one of the pockets of his utility belt and pulled out the blue-and-white miniature airplane Alex had seen in his office.

Under most circumstances, the pocket-sized plane would have seemed like a child's toy, but it was actually much more. The aircraft was a complex, fully functioning machine with the ability to fly inside the human body. It would allow Frank to navigate through Alex's body easily to help fix the parts that were damaged by the cold virus.

"This is what I use to travel," Frank said as he held the tiny plane on the tip of his finger. Then with a small flick, Frank tossed the plane into the air then pressed one of the small square buttons located on his left wrist. In an instant, the plane sailed through the air then immediately stopped and began to hover on its own.

Alex almost erupted with excitement. He couldn't believe what he had seen. A toy-sized plane was now floating by itself in the middle of his bedroom. He was sure he was either having a very strange dream or that his dad had somehow pulled off an unbelievable magic trick. He pinched his hand to make sure he really was awake. Sure enough, he was, and the plane was still floating.

"Okay, here's the plan," Frank continued, "I'm going to shrink and fly into your nose."

With that, Alex gave a look of uncertainty and touched the round ball on the edge of his nose.

Frank noticed and chuckled softly. "It's okay, Al. The blood vessels in the sinuses of your nose have become irritated and swollen because of the virus. That's why it's hard for you to breathe right now. I'm going to start there to relieve your congestion."

Frank's confidence was high, and his positive attitude helped to eliminate any doubts that lingered in Alex's mind. He was a doctor after all and a very good one. He knew just how to put Alex at ease while still explaining what medical procedures he had to perform. After a detailed yet brief explanation, Alex was left feeling assured, excited, but still a little nervous.

Frank tapped another button on his wrist, then his blue-and-white helmet with a clear face shield suddenly appeared and covered his head completely.

"Ready?" Frank yelled through it as he accepted one of the two-way radios from Alex and placed it into his pocket.

"Ready," Alex answered with a huge smile.

Frank reached over to his wrist to press another button, but before he could, Alex shouted at him.

"Wait, what's your superhero name, Dad?"

Frank immediately flashed a smile. "Call me Micro Dad." He leapt into the air as his finger slid across one of the square buttons, and in an instant, he and the micro-plane disappeared.

Chapter 5

The micro-plane glided through the room. It flew effortlessly, and Micro Dad controlled it like an expert pilot. He was full of excitement, doing loops and barrel rolls around Alex's bedroom furniture before finally leveling and continuing to Alex's nose.

Frank had been little Frankie Freeman as a kid. He had dreamed of one day becoming a doctor ever since he could remember. He would stay up late to watch the latest medical TV show while practicing the language with his parents, often asking for "ten ccs of juice, stat". When he turned twelve, he asked for nothing but books about human anatomy, and for the next three months, he drove his two older brothers and younger sister crazy, diagnosing every cough and sneeze they had.

He was thrilled when he finished medical school and began working at Metlife Hospital. All his dreams had come true. He entered the hospital every day with wonderment and passion. There was hardly ever a time when he felt nervous while treating patients with simple or even serious illnesses. He knew being a doctor was his calling and he loved every minute of it. Even now, as Micro Dad, he felt an overwhelming sense of joy as he approached Alex's cavernous nostrils.

The plane slowed to a crawl and began to hover in place before entering. Micro Dad stared at the seemingly endless tunnel and began studying the best way to navigate the forest of nose hairs and slimy mucus without being trapped in it like the millions of other microscopic intruders that attempted to invade

Alex's body on a daily basis. Micro Dad knew the snot would be difficult to fly through, but he couldn't help but marvel at how great the human body was at defending itself and creating obstacles for potentially dangerous creatures, even if that defense was currently thick, green, sticky and blocking his path to the sinuses.

"Micro Dad. Come in, Micro Dad. Are you there?" the two-way radio screeched as Alex's voice came blaring out, breaking Micro Dad's concentration.

"Can you hear me? Does this thing even work? Dad!" Alex yelled then started coughing again.

Micro Dad took it out of his pocket and replied, "I'm here, Alex. What's up?"

"What's your status? Over. Have you made it to my sinuses yet? Over."

"Not yet, Al. I'm not even in your nose yet," Micro Dad answered, still studying his path.

"Well, what's taking so long? Over," Alex asked with an impatient tone.

Micro Dad shook his head and glanced at the radio in his hand with a look of surprise. It had only been a few minutes since he had disappeared, but Alex's patience was already gone.

"These things take time, Alex," he said calmly.

"But we only have a few hours until the science fair, over," Alex said.

"Don't worry, Al. Just relax. I'll have the job done and will be back before you know it," Micro Dad said confidently, "and why do you keep saying 'over' at the end of every sentence?"

"That's what the sidekicks do in all the movies," Alex replied passionately. "We can use other words, too. How 'bout 'Roger, copy that', and 'Mayday' if you need help?"

35

Micro Dad couldn't help but smile at Alex's excitement. "Let's leave the radio communication terms alone for right now," he said with a laugh. "I think I've found the best route, so I'll let you know when I make it there. Try to get some rest, Al."

"Ah, man. Okay," Alex agreed reluctantly, "but call me if you need any help. Any help at all. I'll be right here. The radio is in my hand. Don't hesitate to call. At any time."

Micro Dad chuckled. "Don't worry, partner," he said encouragingly. "I'll keep you posted. Over and out."

There was sudden silence, giving Micro Dad another second to collect his thoughts and prepare for his journey. He gently gripped the plane's throttle and slowly moved it toward his chest. In response, the plane let out a soft hum as it steadily accelerated forwards and straight into Alex's left nostril. It continued to glide smoothly and gracefully as it entered the nose's atmosphere.

He flew quickly yet cautiously, avoiding every obstacle in his path for the first several minutes. Without warning, a tidal wave of disgusting, slimy mucus suddenly trudged toward him, threatening to entrap the micro-plane in its sticky mass like a spider catching prey in its web. He only had seconds to think before he would be caught.

Thinking fast, Micro Dad pressed a small red button which was located directly in front of him. Instantly, two large metal pipes extended from out of the back of the plane. He sat helpless and stared at the avalanche of snot coming toward him and waited, moments from being swallowed up. Suddenly, steam erupted out of the tail pipes, rapidly thrusting the plane forward. It took off like a rocket, pinning Micro Dad to his seat for a brief moment until he was able to grab hold of the controls.

It was just in time. He saw a small gap to the left of the oncoming wave and raced toward it. He knew it would be a tight squeeze, but he was sure he could make it, about seventy-five percent sure, but he knew that would have to do. Unfortunately, the opening shrunk the closer he got.

As time and space ran out, Micro Dad sped along the side of the nostril, making sure to avoid the mucus on the right. But he quickly realized he could no longer maneuver around the forest of hairs to avoid the large mass of snot. He had to fly straight through them. One-by-one, the plane slammed into single strands of hair in its path, causing the micro-plane to shake wildly.

Unsure of just how much more the plane could take, an uneasy feeling began to grow inside Micro Dad until he finally saw the exit nearby. It was close. He just needed a little more time. He continued colliding with wiry hairs and gliding past the blob of mucus when something caught his attention. Trapped in the thick snot were hundreds of lifeless germs encased in the mucus like sprinkles in Jell-O. It was a traveling graveyard.

The mucus was produced by parts of Alex's nose to trap the invading germs. The defensive strategy worked well and ultimately evicted some of the germs by way of a runny nose. Luckily, Alex's immune system had won this battle, but Micro Dad knew there would be plenty more viruses left to fight in the ongoing war with the common cold. He just had to get past the snot.

Moments later, Micro Dad had done it. He had finally made it past the blob of mucus and was closer to reaching the sinuses. Nothing was left to stand in his way. Unexpectedly, the shred of light from outside of the nose disappeared, eclipsed by a large sheeted object, leaving Micro Dad in complete darkness.

The situation immediately dawned on him. The mucus traveling down Alex's nose was a huge obstacle to him but just a runny nose to Alex. That snot had to be removed somehow as

Alex prepared for an intense blow. Micro Dad only had a few seconds before he was violently launched out of Alex's nose and hurled into a waiting piece of tissue.

He flipped a switch to brighten his path and quickly initiated the superspeed feature of the micro-plane. With a press of a button, another burst of steam exploded out of the tail pipes, pushing the plane forward. It rocketed straight ahead. Micro Dad could see the large sign in front of him that pointed in the direction of the sinuses. The plane was only moments away from reaching the entrance when a deafening roar erupted as Alex pinched his nose with the tissue and blew, creating a severe storm worse than anything Micro Dad had seen on the weather channel.

Motionless dust particles suddenly became energized and swirled through the nose wildly. Hairs swayed like trees in a hurricane, disturbed but still firmly rooted in place. The large blob of mucus, once utterly terrifying, was now helpless as it was carried through the air before landing on the awaiting Kleenex, but it had done its job. It took countless germs along with it.

Chapter 6

Alex sat on his bed counting backwards from one thousand. He used the counting trick several times when he was tired but couldn't fall asleep at night, but this time, his brain refused to surrender to the exhaustion his body was feeling. He counted until he made it to three hundred and sixty-eight then quit.

He attempted to do what his dad had said and rest, but he couldn't get his mind to slow down and stop moving a mile a minute. Thoughts of his dad fighting a war inside him and against creatures that could only be seen with a microscope consumed every inch of his brain. He knew the situation was incredibly strange, but it was even more amazing and exciting. Frank was never the coolest dad in the world, but now, Alex thought of him in a different way. Frank was now a superhero, a microscopic bodyguard.

"How many of my friends can say their dad is a superhero?" Alex thought. "I can't wait to see the looks on their faces. But would they even believe me? I can show them. I can bring him to school for career day, and it would be the best one in history!" he schemed but soon began to think sensibly and let his mind drift to other thoughts related to superheroes, like what kind of costume he would wear since he was Micro Dad's new sidekick.

Exhaustion almost overcame him minutes later, but as he lay in bed, he felt a surge of snot rushing down his nose like a flowing stream and pulled himself up to get a tissue from his nightstand. He gave a few harsh blows into it until, feeling satisfied, he stood on his bed and shouted "Three, two, one!" and shot the soggy paper into the metal trashcan across the room. The feeling of fatigue quickly returned, and he clumsily fell back onto the bed, sniffled deeply then continued counting.

"Three hundred and sixty-nine," he said miserably.

It had been half an hour since Micro Dad had vanished into his nose. That was the last time they had spoken. Alex still didn't feel any better and now Micro Dad was missing, so he began to worry. He trusted his dad and knew he would try his best no matter what, but if Micro Dad was missing in action and there were no signs of him getting better then something terrible must have happened.

"What if he's hurt?" Alex thought. "What if the plane stopped working and he's trapped in my nose? He could be in there forever! Unless he's—" Alex's thoughts quickly changed. He suddenly remembered blowing his nose only moments earlier, then his stomach twisted into knots. He felt even sicker, not from his illness but from the fear of his dad being hurt and trapped in a used piece of Kleenex or worse, lost somewhere in his room.

Alex inspected every inch of his bed as quickly as he could. He moved the sheets and pillows very gently and carefully while examining each object. His eyes were as focused as lasers. His face was so close that his nose almost touched every item he inspected.

"Dad, if you're here, don't worry. I'm going to find you," Alex whispered.

If anyone would have come into the room at that moment, Alex would have looked insane, talking softly to himself and closely scanning his bed like a dog searching for a lost bone. He even showed the crazy, animal-like behavior by crawling around in circles as if he were looking for a perfect spot to lie down. He continued the seemingly odd behavior for nearly five minutes until he glanced up at the grey trashcan in the corner of the room.

"The Kleenex!" he yelled loudly.

Then Alex cautiously tip-toed over to it, keeping his heels raised just in case Micro Dad had somehow ended up on the floor. Alex wanted to avoid squashing his dad like a bug. He sat on the floor with his back to the wall and, with a look of disgust, retrieved the wet tissue and inspected it closely.

"This is so gross," he said and continued his inspection, rotating the paper while staring at it intensely. Suddenly, a sharp sound of static screeched out of the radio. Alex scrambled to his feet to find the walkie-talkie. After a few seconds, he found it tucked underneath his pillow. He picked it up and desperately hoped to hear another sound spill out of the speaker. Another shriek erupted moments later, then Micro Dad's voice followed.

"Alex, come in, Alex. Over."

Chapter 7

Micro Dad was lucky to avoid the same fate as the mucus. Even in superspeed, the plane couldn't withstand the force of a blown nose. It had almost made it. The plane was only seconds away from reaching the sinuses when a strong gust of air pushed it backward, sending it spiraling out of control toward Alex's nostrils until eventually crashing hard onto a bed of nose hairs. Micro Dad was thrown to the floor and in an instant, everything around him turned to darkness.

Afterwards, he opened his eyes but only saw black. The plane had lost power on impact and was completely dark inside. Micro Dad rested on the metal floor for a few seconds before he stood up and dusted himself off. To his surprise, he hadn't been injured in the crash. He didn't have any bruises or breaks, but he still felt beaten.

The science fair was starting in just a few short hours, and he still had so much work to do. He hadn't even finished phase one of his mission, and he was already behind schedule. Every minute he lost traveling back through Alex's nose was time he could have spent fixing the sinuses. It was difficult, but Micro Dad refused to quit. He had faced tougher obstacles in his everyday life as a doctor and plenty as a microscopic superhero, so giving up wasn't an option.

With a sudden burst of energy, Micro Dad blindly staggered to the front of the plane until he found his chair. He flopped into it then reached for the controls and flipped the switch to start the plane. It slowly showed signs of life. Red, green and yellow lights from all around the plane began to flash dimly for a few seconds before finally filling the room. Soon after, the plane began to hum, softly at first, but the sound grew louder as the plane began to lift off the bed of hairs and hover into the air.

Micro Dad buckled himself into his seat then pressed the button to start superspeed. In an instant, the micro-plane took off in a blur. It raced back up Alex's nose and reached the sinuses in what felt like seconds.

When the plane landed, Micro Dad took the walkie-talkie out of his utility belt and attempted to call Alex before leaving the safety of the plane and venturing out onto the sinuses. Unfortunately, the radio wouldn't work, and all he could hear was hissing electrical interference. He repeated, "Alex, come in, Alex, over," while pacing back and forth across the plane. He tried holding the radio in every direction above his head, but only the high-pitched squeal of static spilled out of the speaker.

Micro Dad repeated the routine over and over for several minutes until, finally, he heard the pleasant sound of Alex's voice.

"Dad!" Alex shouted. "Are you okay?"

"I'm fine, Al. I've had a few obstacles already, but I'm doing fine and continuing with the mission."

Micro Dad could hear a heavy sigh from the other side of the walkie then Alex's voice once again.

"That's great. Where are you?" he asked.

Micro Dad smiled and stared out of the window. "I just made it to your sinuses."

Alex quickly became cheerful. "You wouldn't believe what I've been through, Dad," he said. "I thought I blew you out of my nose."

Alex then spent the next few minutes describing in vivid detail what had happened with the Kleenex and his search, which had led him to inspecting every inch of his room. Micro Dad just listened without saying a word, smiling the entire time. When he finished, Micro Dad laughed loudly before speaking.

"That's quite a story," he said. "You're one heck of a sidekick."

"I am?" Alex asked, confused. "But how? I almost ruined the mission."

"You blew your nose because you had to. That was your body's way of getting rid of some of the germs that have been making you sick. I was just in the wrong place at the wrong time," Micro Dad explained. "Besides, it sounds like you tried really hard to find me when you thought I was lost."

"I didn't think of it like that," Alex said.. "I guess you're right."

"And just so you know, Al, I'm too small for you to see right now. You would've needed a microscope to see me," Micro Dad said with another laugh as he glanced at the clock in the center of the micro-plane's control panel.

"It looks like time's running out, Al. I have to get to work on these swollen sinuses. I'll have the radio in my belt if you need me, and I'll call you back as soon as I can."

"Roger that, Micro Dad," Alex said excitedly.

Micro Dad placed the walkie in his utility belt and walked over to the large door at the back of the plane. He tapped a button on his wrist, and his helmet reappeared, covering his entire head completely. Then he reached out and pressed a red circular button marked "Exit". In response, the door rose in a slow mechanical motion as stairs suddenly appeared and fell to the surface of the sinuses.

Once the final step landed, Micro Dad walked down each one carefully, studying his surroundings. He stared at the brightly colored surface, in shock at just how badly the cold virus had attacked Alex's sinuses. They were usually a light pink but were now a shade of bright red.

He stepped lightly on the rocky surface when he reached the ground. The sinuses were so badly swollen that every step he took was shaky and unbalanced. It was like walking inside a Moon Bounce. Every step he took was delicate.

Micro Dad continued to examine the scene as he walked across the sinuses. He was surrounded by an enormous hollow opening that hung above him like the walls of a cave. The layer that covered the walls, previously thin and pale, was now red and swollen. It reminded Micro Dad of a room filled with overly inflated red balloons.

Despite the remarkable burst of color, the swelling looked painful. Micro Dad couldn't help but cringe with every step he took. It seemed as if each red mass would burst with the slightest disturbance.

"No wonder Alex's nose is so congested," he thought to himself, "the sinuses aren't normally this red and puffy."

He reached into his utility belt and pulled out seven circular objects. The objects looked like small pearls in his hands, but they were actually a great tool Micro Dad had invented. Each round tablet held a large amount of decongestant. They were small but powerful doses of medicine that would be released as mist when triggered.

Micro Dad liked to call them nose grenades. He loved the invention because each grenade could deliver a strong dose right on the surface of the sinuses and would quickly seep into it, reducing swelling, and therefore congestion, within seconds.

They wouldn't be effective until they were embedded into the surface, however, so Micro Dad had to first arrange them precisely so that a cloud of mist could blanket the entire area of the sinuses. It wasn't a difficult task, but it was sure to take time.

He was lucky to have the time to do his work in peace without being attacked by the viral invaders when he landed, but to his surprise, he was all alone. The virus had damaged the area and moved on, leaving the sinuses as abandoned as a ghost town.

He spent more than half an hour implanting the devices into cracks of the damaged sinuses. Only a small amount of force could set the objects off, so Micro Dad had to handle them with extreme care and move slowly. When the grenades were all planted perfectly, Micro Dad walked back to his plane and strolled up the steps before pressing the glowing red button marked "Enter".

The door let out a soft hiss then slowly rose, stopping once it reached the top of the doorway. He entered then pressed the exit button with the palm of his hand to close the door behind him. Then Micro Dad quickly found his chair and fell into it. He pushed a button on his wrist to remove his helmet. It quickly disappeared, uncovering his head and face.

The helmet was nearly indestructible, but it also made him sweat heavily, so he was glad to have a short break from it. He took a few deep breaths then began to smile brightly. All he had to do now was trigger the nose grenades, sit back and watch the show.

He reached into his utility belt and pulled out a slender aluminum item. It was coated with a shade of silver. There was a black button in the shape of a cylinder on the top of the object which allowed him to click it like a ballpoint pen. The metal item was the detonator for the grenades. With one twitch of his thumb,

Micro Dad pressed it.

In less than a second, a tiny window on each grenade unlocked and opened, releasing a flood of white vapor that poured out and steadily covered the sinuses. The steam hovered just above the surface like a dense fog in the early morning then slowly sank into the membrane and vanished. Less than a minute later, the sinuses began to change. The intense, bright-red hue turned into a calm, light pink, and the mounds of swelling suddenly shrank until only a thin layer remained across every inch of the sinuses.

Step one was now complete.

Chapter 8

Alex sat on his bed and forcefully turned the knobs and pressed the buttons of his wireless video game remote. His friend, Aiden, had given him a new video game a week prior, but he hadn't had time to play it due to homework and countless hours of tirelessly working on his science fair project. Now, however, he decided to take advantage of the free time. It was also a much-needed distraction from his cold and worrying about Micro Dad's progress every second.

He stared at the television screen intensely as his avatar battled a swarm of flesh-eating zombies. He was so focused on the game that he almost forgot that he wasn't actually in a world full of brainless reanimated corpses. He ducked and let out a few howls when the zombies got too close. He even closed his eyes in terror a few times when the creatures unexpectedly attacked with their vicious teeth and claws, nipping at his character's arms and legs. The game was so riveting, he never noticed the tingle in his nose. The feeling was slight at first, but its strength steadily increased.

As he finished another level of the game, warmth began to creep through his nose. Seconds later, more heat formed as if a tiny fire had been lit deep inside. Alex paused the game, set the remote down on the bed, and focused on the strange feeling, unsure of what was happening. It wasn't painful. In fact, it was sort of refreshing.

Alex knew something incredible was happening. Suddenly,

the sensation disappeared. The pressure in his nose began to decrease. Air started to flow through his nostrils freely. After a minute, Alex inhaled deeply then released the breath with a smile. His nose was healed.

Chapter 9

Micro Dad left the sinuses and flew back into the nasal cavity after setting off the nose grenades. There were still jungles of nose hairs to navigate through, but he didn't have any trouble now that the sinuses were fixed, and the waves of snot had all disappeared. He was able to cruise smoothly as he approached the second phase of his mission. Suddenly, Alex's voice erupted out of the radio.

"Micro Dad! Come in, Micro Dad!" he shouted.

Micro Dad removed the walkie from his utility belt and spoke. "Micro Dad here, what's your status, Alex? Over," he said with a smile.

"My nose is fixed!" Alex was full of excitement. "My nose is fixed. I don't know what you did, but it worked."

Micro Dad was thrilled to hear the good news. He spent the next few minutes explaining how the nose grenades worked and how the swelling in his sinuses had disappeared. After the explanation, Alex began sounding more hopeful about his chances of making it to the science fair.

"This is great, but I still have a really bad sore throat, and I'm still coughing like crazy. How are you going to fix those?" asked Alex.

"One step at a time, Al," Micro Dad said. "I'm flying through your nasal cavity now, and I'll reach your sore throat any minute."

Alex seemed confused. "But how will you get to my throat

if you're flying through my nose? My throat is under my nose."

Micro Dad smiled. He always loved teaching, especially about the human body. He could spend hours at home going on and on about his day and the interesting things he had seen while working, until someone in the family, usually Maya, told him to wrap it up.

"There will be a path that connects your nose and throat called the nasopharynx," he began. "I'll be able to cross that path once I reach the back of your nose."

"I still don't understand," Alex responded, sounding skeptical. "My mouth and nose are separate, aren't they?"

"Think of it like a bridge that connects two roads," Micro Dad continued, "I'll be crossing that bridge to get to your sore throat. The nasopharynx is how we are all able to breathe through our noses. The air comes from our lungs, up our throats, past the nasopharynx and out of our noses."

"I never thought about how I breathe," said Alex. "It's not as cool as building machines, but I guess it's cooler than I thought."

Micro Dad grinned. "I know how much you like building things, but think of our bodies like one big machine made up of lots of smaller machines, Al. There are so many parts that work together to help us breathe, eat, and even move. I think it's all pretty cool, but I'm just your nerdy dad," he said with a soft laugh.

After a moment, Alex spoke. "Wow. That's amazing," then he paused for a moment longer. "But what's the plan to fix my throat after you pass the 'naso-pharaoh-linx' bridge thing?"

"Actually, I'm still working on that part. I just crossed the bridge, but I haven't come up with a plan of attack just yet," Micro Dad said almost in a whisper as his voice trailed off.

At that moment, he approached a massive wall at the back

of Alex's mouth. It was as red as a stop sign and contained an endless number of cracks and wounds due to the damage that was done by the virus. Micro Dad felt as if he were staring up at the Grand Canyon, but it was only Alex's sore throat. The color was severe and intense, and its size dwarfed the micro-plane completely.

"Micro Dad, are you still there?" asked Alex.

"Sorry, Al. My mind drifted away for a second. I've made it to your sore throat. It's a lot worse than it seemed this morning."

"Is it too bad for you to fix?" Alex asked with worry in his voice.

"Sure. I can fix it," Micro Dad replied encouragingly, "but it's going to take some work, so I had better get started. I'll check in with you as soon as I can."

"Oh, man, I was hoping to hear more about your plan."

"I may have to wing this one, Al. Besides—"

"I know, I know," Alex interrupted, "I should be resting. Roger that, Micro Dad. Let me know if you need anything."

Micro Dad heard the "click" from the radio then Alex was gone. He placed the walkie back into his pocket and sat motionless and hovered in front of the wall. Alex's throat was even worse than his sinuses had been, so that meant it would take even more time to fix it, and time wasn't something Micro Dad had a lot of. He had been lucky to treat the sinuses without any disturbance from the virus, but he knew the virus was spreading quickly and could attack again at any moment. Sooner or later, he would have to fight.

The virus was destructive, relentless, and would stop at nothing to inflict as much damage as it could on Alex's body. He was known worldwide as the Rhinovirus, but he always liked to be referred to simply as "The Rhino" to scare the white blood cells that tried to stand in his way. The Rhino was small, even for a virus, but his stature was deceptive. He was aggressive and explosive like a tiny firecracker. Anything could set The Rhino off and trigger his rage, especially mentioning his size.

He could go unnoticed inside of people for days until he found the perfect moment to assemble his army. It was made up of his copies, making a large number of them very dangerous. The copies even wore the same unpleasant scowl on their faces and had the same firecracker temper. They were identical in almost every way, except they lacked his intelligence and were mostly mindless and dimwitted. However, what they lacked in intellect they made up for by having an endless hunger to destroy everything in their path.

The Rhino first arrived by riding in on a drop of spit that sprayed out of Sneezing Eddie's mouth when he had sneezed. He rode that mist, and like a light breeze, the droplets glided through the air until they landed inside Alex's nose. Alex, unaware of the intruder, drew in a breath and inhaled the unwanted hitchhiker.

Once inside, The Rhino made his way through Alex's nose and landed on a small bean-shaped structure at the back of the throat called a lymph gland. He hid inside it and waited until he had enough strength to make his copies. After a few days, while Alex's exhausted cells were busy helping him preserve enough energy to go to school and work nights on his science fair project, The Rhino crept back to the nose undetected, under the cover of darkness, and created his first copy by transforming one of Alex's own cells.

The unsuspecting nose cell never saw it coming. It was working hard, pacing back and forth, protecting the nose against intruders, when suddenly, The Rhino attacked. The virus leapt out of the shadows into the air, and as fast as lightning, he reached for the cell. The cell tried to turn and face its attacker, but The Rhino was far too quick. The fight was over before it began.

The Rhino had already taken hold of the cell's arm. His massive hands gripped tightly around it, as if they were covered in glue. There was no escape. The thin cell was left standing helpless and motionless as it felt itself begin to change.

After a few seconds, the cell's eyes turned a milky white, then the transformation began. It started with the cell's feet and traveled up its body. The cell's spotless black boots gradually turned to stained, brown sandals. Its thin, pencil-like legs turned short and bulky, and its crisp, clean pants became a pair of denim jeans covered in holes. The cell's upper body grew wider, leaving behind a round chubby frame.

Next, two beefy arms grew in place of the cell's scrawny limbs, and at the ends of them, two cartoonishly large hands appeared. Even the cell's jacket changed into a filthy t-shirt with a logo in the middle of it that was too faded to make out. It stretched across the cell's large, newly formed chest and even larger gut.

In no time, the cell was unrecognizable. Its soft, smooth, light-pink skin was now grey, rough, and harsh like sandpaper. Its head had doubled in size, and one large white horn emerged in the center of it. The cell was completely gone. What stood in its place was a short, grey virus with a large belly, a massive horn, and empty pale eyes.

The Rhino continued to multiply over and over as quickly as he could. Two Rhinos suddenly became four, and four became many, many more. Within hours, he and his clones had created hundreds of other copies by repeating the same process. Days later, The Rhino had a large, destructive army that ran wild in Alex's body. They battled the cells in his nose and throat and eventually beat them all, causing the painful and irritating symptoms that kept Alex out of school.

Micro Dad knew there would be countless copies by now, and he didn't want to face the swarm unprepared. With precious time ticking away, Micro Dad finally came up with a plan. He got on his feet and rushed over to a metal door located in the floor of the plane. He firmly grabbed the ring-shaped handle and forcefully yanked it upward, opening the door and revealing a hidden compartment. He reached in and pulled out a square box that contained two vital items that would help Micro Dad defeat The Rhino and his copies.

The first item was a shiny, black weapon that looked as if it would be the best option in *Call of Duty*. It was a large military-style weapon with plenty of intimidating accessories and included Micro Dad's stethoscope and thermometer symbol printed on its side. It worked like a paintball gun, which made it simple and easy to use. Instead of balls of paint, however, Micro Dad's gun fired round capsules made of a mixture of sticky syrup and a high dose of the element zinc.

For months, Micro Dad had spent countless hours testing different vitamins and minerals that could stop the cold virus from spreading once it attacked, and after many failures, he had finally discovered zinc's effects. He learned that once zinc was attached, the element could trap the virus and even prevent it from transforming other cells into copies. It was simple. The syrup helped the zinc stick to the virus like gum on the bottom of a shoe while the zinc turned each of them into a lifeless statue with just one touch.

He never tested it, but he was sure it could work, but first, he needed a powerful weapon to shoot the capsules. That's when he created the micro gun. The weapon was electronic and ran on a small but effective battery that fit securely inside the micro gun's frame. Just one tap of the trigger would send a fast-moving signal to the gun's internal controls. In response, a high-powered pellet would shoot out of the weapon with incredibly fast speed and attach itself to a virus before getting to work. The weapon could truly put an end to the viral intruders.

The micro gun would be a game-changer for Micro Dad in his war with The Rhino, but it couldn't heal Alex's cherry-colored throat. The next item in the box could, however. Enclosed in plastic packaging underneath the micro gun were a dozen white disk-shaped objects. They were all about the size of Micro Dad's hand and as flat as pancakes. Micro Dad removed them from the box along with the gun and placed them all on a table in the back of the plane.

The pale, thin objects were an important part of Micro Dad's plan. The disks contained a mixture of ingredients that could make Alex's throat feel better in no time. Honey was the core ingredient and would provide much needed relief for Alex by coating the throat and stopping the dry, scratchy feeling that bothered him so badly. A large amount of lemon juice was also used to rid Alex of his cough. The acid in the lemon juice would destroy any thick mucus that settled in his throat.

The final ingredient was a precise amount of a painkiller. It was like the Novocain dentists use during routine cavity fillings that causes patients to drool like bulldogs. The medication in the disks would numb Alex's throat, blocking the harsh pain he felt.

All three ingredients were a team of sore-throat-stopping power, but they needed to be absorbed into the throat to be effective. The disks were designed to carry each component past the damaged outer layer and into the tissue. They seemed fragile, but each one had a unique ability to be unbreakable until they no longer needed to be. After Micro Dad created the disks, he soaked them in a clear high-tech gel. The gel fused with the disks and the ingredients inside them, making the mixture as hard as steel until they needed to become liquid.

The time had come to test the disks. First, Micro Dad had to attach each one to a different part of Alex's dry, cracked throat. He had a dozen disks and would have to plant them all to cover the large surface of the throat. Unfortunately, he couldn't fly the micro-plane and attach the disks at the same time, so he knew he would have to leave the comfort of the plane again and travel out onto the brightly colored cliff-like structure to perform the mission.

He would have to climb up and across the structure on his own. The climb would be dangerous, not to mention terrifying. He couldn't use any tools because there was a risk of damaging Alex's throat even more. He knew he could slip and fall or get stuck in one of the many open cracks that lay across the surface of the throat. There were an unlimited number of ways something could go wrong, but somehow, Micro Dad remained calm.

He showed no signs of worry or fear. He knew all the risks he was facing and tried not to give them a second thought. He placed the disks into a bag then slung it over his shoulder as he walked over to the front of the plane to disengage autopilot. After a few moments, he took control of the plane and flew closer to the wall of the throat until he found the perfect spot. The plane's lights shined brightly into the darkness, illuminating the vivid reds on the surface that seemed to glow as he got closer to it. When he was close enough, he turned the wheel and slowly reversed backward so that the rear door of the plane was facing the wall, then he reengaged autopilot and stood up to walk to the back of the plane.

Once he reached the door, he pressed a button on his wrist, making his helmet reappear, then pressed the "Exit" button. In response, the door lifted off the ground, letting out soft hisses as the equipment sprang to life. Micro Dad turned and looked around the room. An intense feeling suddenly washed over him. His belly began to grumble and ache, aware of the danger he was facing. He touched it as if to tell it that everything was fine then turned back toward the open doorway and stared out at the menacing wall. The bright color and the cracks throughout its surface seemed to call out to him, daring him to make a move.

He closed his eyes, took a deep breath and jumped.

Chapter 10

Micro Dad's arms and legs flailed wildly as he fell down Alex's throat. He reached out, hoping to grab the nearest gap in the gigantic wall, but his fingers couldn't grip any of the small cracks. Micro Dad's weight pulled him down as if he were skydiving. Flashes of the red wall raced past him. He dropped farther and farther down, helpless to stop himself.

He continued to plummet for what felt like hours until he finally got lucky. He glanced down and saw a break in the skin that was large enough to grab, but he only had a few seconds before he would reach it, so he had to act fast. As he tumbled down, he shot his hand out with incredible speed and with enough power to fit his hand into the open space. In an instant, his body jerked then smashed into the wall forcefully. He trembled from the impact, but he was safe.

Micro Dad hung there, dangling like fruit from a tree. He knew he was lucky to be alive. If he had been just a second slower, he would have continued to fall down the long, dark tunnel of the throat, eventually falling to the stomach, where nothing could escape and where only the meanest bacteria lived. Luckily, he had avoided that fate, at least for that moment.

He stared down at the seemingly endless pit below him and saw nothing but black. The possibility of his hand slipping out of the crack and sending him down into a never-ending darkness quickly entered his mind. He shuddered at the thought. The cold tingle of fear began creeping up his spine. He stared at his hand, unsure of whether it would hold. He knew with one wrong move, he could end up swimming in a pool of stomach acid.

Micro Dad was at the point of no return and only had one option. He had to climb back up the enormous wall, attaching the disks along the way. This was easier said than done, however. It would be difficult to climb the huge, slippery structure while also dodging showers of spit that were sure to come pouring down on him every time Alex swallowed. It would be like climbing up a large waterfall.

Using all his strength, Micro Dad tightened the muscles in his right arm and slowly pulled the rest of his upper body up to meet his elbow. Once his body was high enough, he continued to grip the wall, then he stretched his other arm to reach the closest break in the skin. He struggled for a few seconds, his fingers barely touching the small gap in the wall, but he eventually grasped it. He held on as tightly as he could while planting both of his boots on the surface of the throat.

When he was sure they were both stable, Micro Dad cautiously removed his right hand from its hold on the wall and reached for another section higher up. He quickly grabbed it then removed his left hand and stretched to grab another section of the wall before bringing his feet up to find a secure section for them to rest. The process of reaching with one hand then holding, reaching with the other, holding, then securing a foothold continued again and again. He did it over and over until he was too exhausted to move any further.

He had to take a break or risk every muscle in his body shutting down. His energy was completely spent, but fortunately for him, he chose a great spot to regain his strength. The throat had some swelling, so there were a few lumps across its surface that were large enough for Micro Dad to rest on. The space was only large enough to fit one foot on, so he looked like a blue-and-white flamingo balancing on one leg for a few minutes then switching to the other. It helped him rest each one while keeping his balance on top of the small lump.

It took a while for him to regain his strength. His previously tired, aching muscles became restored. His stiff, throbbing hands soon loosened, and the pain subsided. Energy grew inside him, helping him finish his climb.

Micro Dad reached out to grab a gap in the wall above him, but suddenly, a flood of water came rushing down. It seemed to appear from out of nowhere and was directly above him in an instant. He barely had time to react. He quickly turned his back to the wall just in time to pin himself to it just as the water roared past, spraying mist in all directions, and threatening to knock him off his perch. As he watched, Micro Dad could only think of the huge green snot that had almost pulled him out of Alex's nose at the start of his journey, but this time was different. This time, Alex's body had a thin, watery liquid known as spit to carry him away.

Alex's body created the saliva to help him swallow food more easily. Its purpose was to break down food into smaller pieces before moving to the stomach. The liquid was also able to kill invading germs by trapping and destroying them. Unfortunately for Micro Dad, he was in the way, yet again, and was witnessing Alex's body at work.

It took several seconds for the flood to stop. Micro Dad had been hit with a few drops, but he was unharmed. He slowly turned to face the wall and restart his climb when his right leg, the only one keeping him upright, slipped on the soaked lump. His body stiffened as he slid to the right, but he caught himself before he could fall.

The wall was coated with the liquid. Micro Dad was barely able to climb the massive structure when it was drier, so now that it was even smoother, his chances of making it up were low. But he wasn't discouraged. He knew that the clock was still ticking to get Alex to the science fair, so he took a deep breath and went for it.

He reached for another gap and gripped it tightly then firmly planted his foot on the ledge and pushed. His body shot up as he grabbed another space and held onto it. With both hands gripping the wall, Micro Dad raised his legs and attempted to plant the bottom of his boots on the throat's surface and do a slow walk upward, but it was too soaked. His feet kept sliding. After several minutes, he had made no progress. He knew he had to change his strategy.

So, he decided to swing instead. Letting his feet slide back down, Micro Dad positioned his left foot on the lump below him and kicked off to the right side. As his body drifted, he swung his right arm out, being sure to keep his left hand attached to the crack that it held, then grabbed another section of the wall. He hung there in the shape of an "X" then brought his legs over. He didn't have much space to stand, so he stood on the balls of his feet so only his toes kept him rooted to the tiny hump on the surface. It was difficult and extremely painful, but he managed to bring his left arm over and held both arms directly above his head.

There were a few more hill-like lumps resting one after another on the surface to Micro Dad's right. He performed the same acrobatic routine, going farther in the same direction. His plan was to keep going until he reached an area that was free from wetness and would allow him to travel up the wall. He needed to go up just a bit more until he reached the center of the sore throat.

He just had to make it back to the micro-plane, which floated near the perfect spot that he chose. Once there, he could start planting the disks then continue to the next step of his mission.

As Micro Dad traveled farther, swinging from one crack to another like a kid playing on monkey bars, he finally found the dry area he had been hoping for. He began climbing the wall intensely, afraid another downpour of saliva would rain on him at any moment. He went up with incredible speed. There was no time to be slow and steady. He was still aware that something could go wrong at any moment, but he threw caution to the wind.

Within just a few minutes, Micro Dad closed in on his destination. He could see the lights from the plane as it hovered in the air. The light illuminated Alex's intense red throat, reminding him of how important it was to get up there and continue working. It was like a flag marking the finish line, and he was overjoyed when he finally reached it.

He had never been so happy to see the micro-plane. Somehow, it was safe and sound. It only had a little extra gloss it had received from the wash of spit.

The glow from the plane lit up the enormous wall like searchlights at a movie premiere, giving Micro Dad plenty of light to work. With one hand rooted securely to the wall, he reached over his shoulder and removed the bag with the disks. He carefully took out one of the thin, pale objects. The disk was as thin as a sheet of paper and weighed next to nothing in Micro Dad's hand. He carefully gripped it, being very careful not to let it slip from his hand, and gently placed it on the surface of the throat.

The pale disk lay against the inflamed red surface of the throat without doing much of anything. Micro Dad stared at it intensely as if to make it work immediately. He had never used the disks before, so he was eager to see them in action. They had worked great in the lab. The tests that were performed had all turned out well, so he was confident that they would work, but he also knew that testing the disks in a lab was completely different from using them on a sore throat in real life.

Minutes went by, and his impatience grew as he continued to wait for something to happen.

"Maybe I did something wrong," he thought to himself then started going over the recipe for the disks. He was sure he had used the right ingredients and the right amounts, but he couldn't understand why it wasn't working.

"Maybe it's just a dud," he said out loud after a few seconds. "I have to try the others."

Micro Dad threw the bag back over his shoulder and prepared to climb even higher to plant another disc. As he gripped the wall and steadied himself, he glanced at the disk stuck to the rocky surface below him. A single, small line had mysteriously appeared directly in the middle of the thin sheet, splitting it in half. Suddenly, the line started to multiply. Within seconds, an endless number of lines shot out in all directions like roots extending from the bottom of a tree. The disk looked as if it had been smashed with a hammer, leaving dozens of little pieces scattered across the section of the wall.

The backdrop of the throat's red surface mixed with the pale, irregular shapes of the broken disk was like a piece of abstract art. Slowly, broken pieces of the disk started to melt like ice cream in the summer, but instead of dripping down the wall, each piece began to form into a thick, sticky substance like silly putty. Micro Dad just stared at the transformation with amazement, completely unaware of what would happen next.

The disk fragments seemed to have a mind of their own.

Micro Dad watched as one fragment slithered as if it were a gooey slug. It crawled to a crack in the wall then turned to liquid again before dissolving into it like a sponge soaking up water. Each slug-like object underwent the same change, and within a few seconds, the dozens of disk pieces all disappeared into the wall of the throat.

Micro Dad was thrilled. He just had to wait a little longer for the ingredients in the disk to do their part and heal Alex's throat. He wasn't sure if it would take seconds or minutes for the disk to work, but he knew that he would know when it did.

Feeling energized, Micro Dad climbed up the wall until he reached a section that was even more dried out and inflamed than the first. When he placed the sheet on the wall this time, the disk shattered and began to dissolve immediately. In less than a minute after planting it, the disk soaked into the throat and vanished.

Micro Dad climbed up and across the wall ten more times until all the disks were planted. The same result occurred each time. The disks attached, formed into slimy, animal-like objects then seeped into the wall, but nothing happened to Alex's throat even when the last disk was gone. Everywhere Micro Dad could see was still as red as a ripened tomato, swollen, and cracked. Micro Dad began to realize that his only chance to heal Alex's throat didn't work.

His eyes fell on the wall. He just needed a sign, any signal that the disks were working and weren't complete duds. His emotions were a combination of excitement, concern, and panic all rolled into one as he gazed out at it. He was sure, at least mostly, that he would see a change at any moment, but time continued to pass and still nothing happened.

His shoulders and back began to ache horribly from hanging

in one place for so long. His hands and fingers were numb, and his legs were incredibly sore. They felt like they were going to unhook themselves from his body and walk away on their own to rest. He knew the pain was his body's way of telling him that he was exhausted and to move on and continue with the mission.

"Are you planning on staying here and looking at the wall all day? There's nothing left for you to do! If you don't come down on your own, then we'll just have to make you come down," he almost heard his tired arms shouting at him.

After a few more seconds, Micro Dad finally listened to his aching body and started to climb down to the micro-plane. He was unbelievably tired. He was more exhausted than he could remember ever being on any other mission, even though there were many that had challenged him.

As he made his way down, he thought about his mission years before when Camille and Alex both had pinkeye at the same time. Micro Dad had had a tough time battling the virus that made them sick, while Frank had had a tough time caring for Camille, who was an extremely difficult patient. She was famous for ignoring all of Frank's professional advice and refused to stay in bed and relax. She understood that her husband was a doctor and knew how to help, but she was too stubborn and too busy with her new marketing project for her job to listen. Every time he had gone to check on her, the soup and orange juice he had given her remained untouched on their nightstand, and she sat in bed almost blind and squinted at her laptop with red, swollen, crust-filled eyes.

It had taken hours for her exhaustion to wear her down and put her to sleep so that Micro Dad was finally able to help her and fight off the infection. When she woke up, Camille had been amazed at how great she felt. She could see perfectly and no longer felt sick. Less than a minute later, she went right back to work as if she had never been sick. Frank couldn't help but smile at his tough, determined wife that day.

The pinkeye mission had been difficult, but Micro Dad's current one was already very challenging. As he got closer, he could see the welcoming sight of the plane's front door, so he began to climb even faster. He was able to reach the doorway within seconds, but once he was in front of it, Micro Dad realized he had one more problem to face. He had to get back in the micro-plane.

It hovered close by the spot Micro Dad stood on the wall but too far for him to enter easily. He tried to reach out and grab the bottom of the plane's doorway while tightly holding onto a piece of the wall with his other hand, but his arm wasn't long enough to reach, and the farther he stretched, the closer he came to losing his grip. After several attempts, Micro Dad finally gave up and thought of a better plan. He tapped a button on his wrist and watched as the bottom of the plane started to move.

A flat square object that looked like a sheet of poster board slowly appeared from a narrow space underneath the plane as if it were a disc being ejected from an Xbox. It was shiny metal and reflected the brightly colored wall that towered in front of it. The metal sheet quickly unfolded into many and became stairs that fell one after another toward Micro Dad. The last step dropped directly in front of him, almost crashing into his chest.

He easily grabbed it and lifted himself up. He carefully climbed the steps and entered the plane. The door closed behind him as he removed his helmet with a press of a button then found his seat in front of the large window in the cockpit and collapsed into it. His faced was drenched in sweat, and he was so tired that all he could think about was sleep. He fought hard to stay awake, but his eyelids fought back even harder and were starting to close shut when something caught his attention.

All around him, Alex's throat was changing. Each round lump Micro Dad had previously used as footholds slowly shrank. The countless number of cracks that were scattered all over the wall like tunnels in an ant farm became thinner and thinner. The wall's bright color that acted like a stop sign, warning Micro Dad about the danger that was all around him, gradually faded. The intense red glow changed to a dim pink in seconds. Every part of Alex's throat began to look healthy and new, which meant no more pain and soreness.

"The disks worked!" Micro Dad shouted. He waved his arms and pumped his fists in the air, suddenly awake and full of energy.

He stared out at the changing scenery with amazement.

"I have to call Alex and see how he's feeling. He's probably jumping through the roof," he said with excitement.

He removed the radio from his utility belt pocket and put it to his lips but just before speaking, he stopped and set it down on the plane's control panel in front of him. He was excited to check on Alex, but he knew he wouldn't be able to continue with the mission if he didn't act fast. The dozens of cracks covering the throat were growing smaller by the second, and Micro Dad had to pass through one of them before they all closed for good. If he didn't, there would be no way for him to get into Alex's bloodstream and help fight The Rhino and his copies. Every second was crucial.

Micro Dad quickly disengaged autopilot and initiated super-speed. Then he gripped the plane's controls and yanked them back, forcing it to sail toward the other side of the throat. The plane picked up speed with every passing moment until it was nearly a shadow, a dark blur making its way closer and closer to the wall. Micro Dad could see flashes of the pink canyon with spots of red on both sides of him as he raced by, but his gaze stayed fixed straight ahead. He had to focus on finding the perfect target.

The cracks continued closing one after another, creating smooth, fresh surfaces. As one shut, Micro Dad changed his focus to another, hoping to choose the right one. He was only moments away from reaching the wall when he finally found the perfect gap he could use to enter before it closed and ended Micro Dad's mission and Alex's chances of going to the science fair.

The crack was closing slower than the rest and was barely wide enough for the plane to fit through, but he continued on. The micro-plane sped up even more and zoomed toward the shrinking line in the wall. Micro Dad reached for a round knob in the center of the plane's control panel and quickly turned it all the way to the left as far as it could go. Next to the knob, there were two blue square buttons with white arrows on them. The first had a small arrow pointing down, and the second had a larger arrow pointing up. Micro Dad placed his hand over the button with the small arrow but didn't press it. He waited for the right moment.

The opening was now even smaller than it had been only seconds before, but it still hadn't closed completely. He kept his hand over the button and waited as time seemed to slow to a crawl. As the plane got closer to the wall, Micro Dad began to count down.

"Three," he said softly as the two sides of the gap began to connect, threatening to flatten the plane like a potato chip.

"Two," Micro Dad said even louder. His heart began to pound like a drum as the plane approached its target, now so close he could reach out and touch it.

"One!" he yelled then hit the blue button as hard as he could just before the micro-plane crashed into the wall.

In a flash, the plane shrank to an even smaller size but continued to fly, speeding past the closing gap, out the other side and into the bloodstream.

Chapter 11

Completely bored, Alex rested in bed and stared up at his rotating ceiling fan. Once again, he had attempted to sleep but was still far too excited, so instead, he spent five minutes watching the blades of the fan spin in circles without blinking, hoping it would hypnotize him into a nap. It didn't work. It just made his eyes so dry that he didn't know if he had stopped blinking because he was actually becoming hypnotized or because his eyes had frozen in place.

The spell finally broke when Alex heard the sound of buzzing coming from across the room. He got out of bed and found his cellphone vibrating wildly on top of his dresser, as if it were excited to bring him messages. He hadn't checked it all day and was surprised to see he had received fifteen new messages and five missed calls. The missed calls were all from his mom, Camille. She had even sent him three texts.

Her first message asked how he was feeling, the second was to make sure he was resting, and the third was to remind him of how much she loved him. The last message she sent pretty much every day, and it was always followed by plenty of hearts and red lips to imply she was kissing him. It made Alex cringe with embarrassment every time, even when he was all alone in his room.

He had asked her to stop sending the messages countless times because she was treating him like a baby and he was basically an adult, to which she always replied, "I don't care how old you are, you'll always be my baby." He knew it would never change, but deep down, and of course he would never admit it, he kind of liked it.

Alex ignored his mom's messages and skipped to the next few. Most of the messages were from his friends, Aiden and Josh, and went:

"You not comin' to school today, bro?" – Aiden

"You should've said you were skippin' today. I would've tried to skip, too... I probably wouldn't have because my mom would kill me, but I would've wanted to." – Josh

"You do the geography homework for Mr. Bradley's class... Can I see it?" – Aiden

"Mrs. Bryant asked about you earlier. Are you skippin' the science fair? You know it's today, right?" – Josh

"Dude, I didn't do my geo homework again. Mr. Bradley kept me after class to talk to me and you know how bad his breath is... I was turning blue from holding my breath for so long... I almost died." – Aiden

"You comin' to school or what? I know you not worried about Zoey." – Josh

"Did you know we were having a math test today?" – Aiden

"How do you find the area of a triangle?" – Aiden

"Well... I failed it." – Aiden

Alex laughed as he read each message from his friends. He saw them every day. They rode the bus together, had classes together and hung out together after school most days. Frank even told people he had four kids because Aiden and Josh were at his house so much. Alex was hardly ever without his best friends, so he hated missing school and not being able to be with them. The three of them had known each other for as long as they could remember.

They had met in kindergarten the day Zoey ruined Alex's cow drawing. Josh and Aiden sat next to Alex and helped cheer him up afterward. Josh helped him draw an even better picture of a rocket ship flying over the moon while Aiden made them both laugh by making fart noises with his mouth until their teacher had enough and made him stop. They had been inseparable ever since.

Josh was a few months younger than the other two but was always the grown-up in the group. He was twelve going on thirty. Whenever Alex and Aiden planned to do something that could get them into trouble, it was always Josh who talked them out of it or gave them an "I told you so" if they didn't listen.

The "I told you so" was almost always saved for Aiden because he seemed to find trouble almost daily. He had the bad habit of saying everything that popped into his head no matter where he was or who the person he was talking to. Like the time a fly hovered around their third-grade teacher, Mrs. Fisch, for ten minutes, so Aiden asked her if she had showered because flies only hovered around things that were dirty and smelled bad. Aiden's parents had a talk with him about politeness that night. He didn't mean to be rude, but since the words had entered his brain, he had to say them. He just couldn't help himself.

They were a crew. Josh was the voice of reason, Aiden the talkative, energetic one, and Alex was the bookworm, who often sat quietly with his head in a book if he wasn't out building something or going off on adventures with his friends. Their messages made Alex think more about Micro Dad. He hoped his dad was still making progress fighting his cold so he could make it to school.

After reading the messages from his friends, Alex scrolled to the last three, that were unread. They were all from Zoey and instantly ruined his mood. A large scowl pushed away his smile. His eyes narrowed and his face twisted as he read the first message.

They began, "Hi, Alex. Missed you in class this morning."

73

Followed by, "Hey, Alex. Hope you're doing okay and not backing out of the science fair…"

Lastly, "I knew you were scared to lose, but I didn't think you would skip school just to avoid getting beat by me again… And guess what? I got a ninety-nine percentage on our math test today." She had even added a smiley face at the end of the sentence just to rub it in.

Alex was furious. He threw his phone down in anger. It landed on the bed with a soft thump then sank into a pillow.

"She thinks I'm scared to lose to her!" he growled, "I'll show her. I'm getting to that science fair no matter what."

He ran to his closet and grabbed a pair of pants and a clean t-shirt. In his rush, he chose a pair of pants that were three sizes too small as well as a t-shirt that his mom had made him that had a picture of Alex sitting on the potty when he was two years old printed on it. He threw them both on, muttering as he struggled to pull up the pants. He grabbed a clean pair of sneakers and sat on his bed to put them on. He quickly jumped and began pacing back and forth while his eyes darted around the room.

He spotted his phone resting on the pillow and rushed to grab it. When he opened it, Zoey's messages returned onto the screen. Alex immediately began writing one of his own. His thumbs tapped the keyboard in quick, jerky motions as if they were racing to see which one could finish first. When he was finished, he smiled and read the messages out loud.

"Don't worry, Zoey. I'll be there. I've just been putting the finishing touches on my project. It'll beat anything you could ever dream of. Get ready to lose."

He ended the message with a winking smiley face next to a pair of boxing gloves then pressed send. Right away, he saw three dots appear, indicating Zoey was typing. After a few seconds, his phone vibrated, and Zoey's message flashed on the screen.

All it said was "Ha Ha Ha" followed by a cartoon version of

her own face. Even in the animation she smiled a toothy grin, showing every bit of her braces.

Alex shouted in anger then quickly braced himself for another coughing fit, but nothing happened. He didn't cough at all, not even a little. He cleared his throat to test it once again, and to his surprise, it was no longer dry and scratchy. The pain he had felt all morning had completely disappeared.

"Micro Dad did it!" he said, excitement replacing the anger inside him.

He wanted to run to the walkie and call Micro Dad, but before he took a step, he hesitated.

"I should just go to school now," he thought to himself. "I mean, I'm mostly better and there's no telling how much longer Micro Dad will take to beat the virus. I can't wait to see Zoey's face when I show up to class."

He grabbed his bookbag off the floor and walked towards the door. He reached out to open it but stopped before his hand could touch the knob. Something made him change his mind. He knew what his dad would say about getting other people sick, and he didn't want to take that chance, even if it meant he'd miss the science fair.

Alex silently stepped away from the door. As he moved back, he caught a glimpse of himself in the mirror beside him. His head snapped back to look at himself. He stared in complete disbelief. His eyes traveled from his tight-fitting pants to his embarrassing shirt.

"What am I wearing?"

Chapter 12

Micro Dad flew past the wall quickly. The worst was over, so he reset the micro-plane to its previous size and continued flying. He had narrowly avoided being crushed by Alex's newly healed throat and was now somewhere in the neck preparing to enter a superhighway, known as a vein, that would lead straight to Alex's lungs. These slender tubes were scattered in all directions throughout Alex's body like spider webs, carrying blood without oxygen to the heart. The blood then travels to the lungs to pick up the oxygen before delivering it to the rest of the body.

The Rhino liked to hide out in the lungs because he always said they were very airy and comfortable, but he was never a very good guest. He would wreck the place, causing pain and damage to the lungs every time. Micro Dad knew where The Rhino would be, so he decided to go right to him.

There were only a few items left to accomplish for Micro Dad to be sure that it would be safe for Alex to go back to school without getting any of his classmates sick. He knew Alex was growing more impatient by the minute and would think about making his escape soon now that his nose and throat felt better. Micro Dad only hoped that he still had enough patience to stay home long enough for him to finish his work and beat The Rhino. After a moment, he decided to call Alex.

"I should check on him and make sure he isn't on his way to school," he said.

But before he could reach for the radio, the vein's ten-lane superhighway came into view. It was jam-packed with endless rows of red blood cells traveling in each of the lanes. They all shouted from their cars and trucks while they beeped their horns relentlessly in a sea of noise. They were all working. Each of their vehicles was full of waste, like carbon dioxide, that they were waiting to take to the lungs to be shipped out of Alex's body. Unfortunately, it was rush hour and the traffic in the vein was terrible. The cells were all at a standstill.

Micro Dad was lucky enough to avoid the traffic. Once he reached the highway, he gripped the plane's controls and flew higher and higher to get well above the road. The plane climbed then leveled off before turning and flying in the same direction as all the blood cells. He went unnoticed for several minutes before a few motionless cells spotted the large aircraft soaring above them all.

Within moments, the highway became quiet. The blood cells all stopped shouting at each other and instead, they stared up at the micro-plane. They pointed their fingers with terror shown on their faces. Whispers traveled from car to car until the entire highway sounded like a beehive.

Whispers such as, "What is that?" and "Do you see that?" slowly began to grow louder then became replaced with, "It's an alien!" and "We need to get out of here!"

Suddenly, panic erupted. Blood cells pressed their car horns again and again in fear, letting out long endless honks. Some fled their cars altogether and ran down the highway screaming while others revved up their engines and prepared to crash through the traffic until they made it to safety. None of them had any idea who Micro Dad was and why he was there.

Chaos followed. Micro Dad stared down at the thousands of cells, completely unaware that he was the cause of the mayhem.

He didn't figure it out until he noticed more and more cells pointing directly at him and the plane.

"Oops," he said with a guilty smile as if he had accidentally spilled a glass of milk instead of scaring thousands of hard-working red blood cells into a panic.

"I had better hurry up and get out of here," Micro Dad said as he gripped the switch to engage superspeed, but before he could start it, he heard a roaring boom from outside of the micro-plane.

He quickly gazed down at the cells on the highway, confused as to what could have made the deafening sound. He noticed every cell had stopped screaming and panicking. Instead, they were all cheering. He couldn't hear the words that came with the cheers, but he knew that the red cells were no longer frightened.

The cells exploded with applause. Some clapped and shouted while hanging from their car windows, while others danced in the middle of the street. Smiles were stuck to each of their faces. They were full of excitement as they continued to stare up towards the sky but not at the micro-plane.

Unexpectedly, three identical sleek white planes zoomed past the crowd of spectators and raced straight toward the micro-plane. They flew in the shape of a "V" with one plane leading while the others followed closely behind. The two trailing aircraft had a pair of missiles attached underneath their bellies while the lead craft only had one remaining. The other had already been fired at Micro Dad.

"Oh no," Micro Dad said with a shaky voice as he turned and saw the approaching aircraft. "Not these guys."

The planes were piloted by some of Alex's greatest white blood cells. They were called neutrophils. The neutrophils were Alex's first line of defense against invading germs. They had one job and one job only: find and destroy anything that ever invaded. They were the best of the best when it came to protecting Alex.

Neutrophils were tough and took their jobs very seriously, usually too seriously, which meant they weren't the nicest cells to be around. They never smiled or laughed. Their faces only knew one position and that was rock solid with minimal expression. At parties, they never danced or sang songs like the rest of the cells. They always stood, never sat, upright in one place and told war stories about how they had shot down hundreds of bacteria or other dangerous enemies. They meant harm to every germ they ever met, and Micro Dad was now that germ.

The planes each had a pair of thin wings that bent backward. They looked like a trio of dive-bombing birds. Shiny, bubble-shaped domes covered the tops of them and looked like one-way mirrors, which made it nearly impossible to see inside. They approached Micro Dad's plane quickly and were directly behind him in seconds. To Micro Dad's surprise, a loud voice roared out of a speaker attached to the lead plane.

"You've entered restricted airspace," the voice said in a robotic tone. "Land your vehicle now and you will be taken into custody. We have fired a warning shot. You will not get another. If you do not comply within five seconds, you will be shot down."

Micro Dad briefly hesitated. "These guys sound pretty serious." He thought then reached for the superspeed switch and prepared to launch. "But I've come too far and don't have time to stop now."

Five seconds passed in an instant. Micro Dad waited for any sign of an attack, but it didn't come. Instead, the three aircraft slowed down and fell further behind the micro-plane as if they were giving up or just having fun with him.

"Maybe they changed their minds," he said with a nervous, awkward laugh.

He glanced back and saw a thin black missile hurtling towards him. It nearly struck the right side of his plane, but Micro Dad turned just in time so that the missile flew forward until it exploded near the top of the vein. The blast was far enough away that it didn't cause any damage to the micro-plane, but it was powerful and made it and Micro Dad shake. He rattled in his seat from the blast and trembled in his bones at the thought that the plane had almost been destroyed. He immediately pressed the button to launch superspeed.

His plane shot off like a spooked gazelle escaping a cheetah. In just seconds, the plane was well out of range of the cells' missiles. He looked back and saw the three ships in the distance.

Micro Dad smiled and let out a sigh of relief.

"That was easy. Maybe too easy. They're supposed to be this super army, and I beat them just like that," he said with a snap of his fingers.

He turned to see the white blood cells disappear from his view, but to his surprise, the three planes had caught up to him and were right behind him, yet again. Micro Dad almost jumped out of his skin. As quickly as his confidence grew, it faded even quicker.

Suddenly, a shower of bullets sprayed out of the front of all three planes and into the micro-plane. Pellets crashed inside and flew in every direction, hitting the table, chairs, and even the food that was in the cabinet. A tiny bag of chips, an apple, and a box of chocolate snack cakes were torn to pieces and fell to the floor. Micro Dad just lowered his head and continued to fly.

"I was looking forward to eating those," he said through

clenched teeth.

Bullets continued to pierce the micro-plane. Soon after, plasma began to ooze into it through the round holes sprinkled across its sides. Micro Dad turned to see the tiny droplets falling to the floor, then he immediately reached out and smashed a button in the center of the control panel. In seconds, a new layer of metal appeared, sealing the holes, and stopping the plasma from entering.

Certain the leaks were sealed, Micro Dad gripped the controls tighter and kept flying. He swerved from left to right to try to avoid the ongoing assault, but nothing he did seemed to work. He tried a few moves to lose them, but he was in the open and was an easy target. The micro-plane was a bit faster than the white cells, so he sped up just enough to gain more distance and pause the hailstorm of bullets.

The cells stopped their attack for a moment, but they seemed to have no plans of slowing down or letting Micro Dad go. They stayed on the plane's tail, flying in perfect formation. The three aircraft flew like one single unit. Every move was made together and at the exact same time. They were like a school of fish swimming in the ocean.

When Micro Dad flew right or left, the white blood cells were behind him like a shadow. Micro Dad's heart began to thump hard in his chest. He didn't know how much longer he or his plane could last. The micro-plane was on the edge of getting obliterated, but there was nothing Micro Dad could do.

Luckily, the bridge to the lungs came into view in front of him. He looked down to the street below and could see that three red blood cells had gotten into an accident and were waiting for the team of lysosomes to clean up the mess littered on the street. They were the reason for the traffic jam throughout the vein.

"The bridge!" he yelled. "Finally. I know I can lose them in the lungs. I just have to make it."

He pushed the controls down firmly and forced the aircraft into a dive toward the road, but before reaching it, he suddenly pulled up, and the plane leveled out just above it. The cells followed without hesitation. They showed no sign of slowing their chase. With them on his tail, Micro Dad approached the bridge then suddenly thought of a plan.

The micro-plane nearly grazed the tops of several cars parked on the bridge as he flew. Red blood cells instantly panicked. They leapt out of their cars and raced up the road to the lungs or back down in the direction they had just come.

Micro Dad held onto the controls, keeping the plane level and parallel to the cars. The plane's belly nearly kissed every one of them. He glanced back to see that the three neutrophils were doing the same, following closely behind him. Without warning, the lead pilot opened fire on the micro-plane.

Bullets tore through the plane's thick metal. Every shot landed, leaving dozens of holes in its battered tail. They were still too far away from the entrance of the lungs for Micro Dad to lose them. He remained an easy target and knew that he would be destroyed quickly if he didn't act fast.

But seconds passed without another shot being fired. The lead plane continued to chase, but suddenly, the two wings broke free from their formation, and with a sudden burst of speed, they sailed forward. Micro Dad watched as the cells reached the micro-plane, boxing him in on each side. He was only able to fly straight ahead.

His eyes darted left and right as he watched the two neutrophils inch closer to the micro-plane. They moved slowly, taking their time to meet it. At the last moment, they rolled their craft just slightly toward the micro-plane so their wings could fall underneath it. Then, they quickly corrected them, causing the tops of each of their wings to collide with the bottom of the micro-plane.

The collision was light. It was barely enough for Micro Dad to feel, but it caused the three planes to connect at their wings. Micro Dad turned his wheel left to right to break away, but he couldn't shake them loose. They flew over the bridge as if the two neutrophils were teaching Micro Dad how to fly with one guide on each wing.

The lead cell continued to fly closely behind. Once it was clear that the micro-plane was restrained, it crept toward its tail. Its aircraft inched forward until its nose was only an arm's reach away, but it avoided ramming it. Instead, it flew just close enough to make its presence known as if it were escorting the plane away.

Micro Dad had nowhere to go. They were getting closer to the lungs. He could even see barricades with armed guards posted at its border. He wasn't going to make it. The two craft began to fly higher, slowly lifting his plane away from the cars and bridge below as they moved.

The micro-plane was trapped. Micro Dad no longer had any control of its movements. He sat helpless and watched as he began to fly higher into the air. His teeth clenched and his grip tightened around the steering wheel, hoping to find a way out.

His eyes ran across the buttons displayed on the control panel in front of him. There were so many, he couldn't decide which to press. His heart pounded like a large drum, and his mind raced as he considered his options. He looked at one button then the next. He only had one chance, and if he chose wrong, he was sure to be taken prisoner by the white cells.

Valuable seconds passed before he finally decided. He

reached for the square button above him and slammed the palm of his hand into it. His body stiffened, preparing for the impact that was sure to follow.

Once the button was pressed, a bright flash immediately erupted from the micro-plane. The beam of light instantly stunned the three neutrophils. The lead plane backed away in a hurry, creating a large gap between it and the micro-plane. The other two white cells panicked and slowly rolled their aircraft inward. Their wings remained locked underneath the micro-plane's as they turned, but within a split second, the bright light faded, revealing only empty space where the micro-plane once was.

The micro-plane had disappeared. Without it as a crutch, the aircraft were instantly forced closer together. The ends of their wings nearly collided into each other, but at the last second, the pilots clumsily pulled their controls back, steering them in opposite directions. They avoided the crash, but the sudden jolt caused the planes to sail out of control toward the walls on both sides of the bridge.

The aircraft both twisted through the air until they came crashing into the barriers that separated the top of the bridge from the seemingly endless space below it. Upon impact, they immediately turned into balls of smoke and flames. Luckily, both pilots were saved because all white blood cells' planes were equipped with automatic ejection seats in case of emergencies, so the neutrophils were quickly launched out of them before the crashes. They floated through the air while dangling from parachutes until they were eventually pushed farther down the highway and away from the lungs.

The micro-plane had shrunk down by five times the size of its pursuers to escape them. Once it was free, Micro Dad hurriedly pushed the wheel forward and forced the plane back down toward the highway. There was a large red truck parked below him, so he dove and flew underneath it. The truck's size hid the micro-plane well, shielding it from the lead neutrophil, which was sure to still be on the hunt.

Micro Dad zoomed past the truck. He still had a long way to go before reaching the lung's entrance, so he used the other abandoned cars for cover. He flew underneath them one by one, zigzagging as he raced along the road in a blur. It seemed as if he would go undetected the rest of the way, but suddenly, as he cruised underneath a gigantic fourteen-wheeled truck, a deafening explosion erupted somewhere above him. Less than a second later, the truck lifted off the ground and sailed into the air, exposing the micro-plane completely.

Immediately, Micro Dad turned to see the last remaining neutrophil hovering over him. Somehow, he had been found. The pilot had fired its last missile at the truck to uncover the now tiny micro-plane. The explosion smashed the truck into pieces, flinging broken parts in every direction.

Micro Dad turned back just in time to see a shadow from one of the truck's large tires cast in front of him. He had no time to react before the plane crashed into it. All he could do was turn the plane's steering wheel as hard as he could to the right while pushing it down to force the plane into a dive. The tire sped past him in the blink of an eye, but as the micro-plane sailed below it, narrowly escaping, it scraped the tip of the plane's left wing.

The bump had just enough force to send the micro-plane sailing toward the ground like an asteroid. The steering wheel shook violently in Micro Dad's hands as he attempted to gain control of the aircraft, but it was no use. The impact was too much for him and his plane. He shut his eyes and braced himself as it plummeted to the ground.

The plane's belly landed first. It bounced off the hard surface again and again for what felt like hours before skidding along the road. When it finally stopped, the entire plane had lost all power, and it had traveled down the length of the highway. It was now only a few cars away from the lung's entrance.

Micro Dad opened his eyes to see complete darkness inside the cockpit. The only available light streamed through the windshield from the vein. He checked himself for injuries but found himself unharmed. Seeing how close he was to the lungs, he pressed several buttons to wake the micro-plane, but nothing worked. The plane just lay lifeless in the middle of the highway.

Suddenly, Micro Dad heard a deep robotic voice ring out above him.

"You, in the vehicle. Do not move or attempt to flee. I have you surrounded. As a protector of the city of Alex, I am placing you under arrest. Step out of your vehicle with your hands up."

The voice sent a chill up Micro Dad's spine. He looked out of his window and saw a pale, thin neutrophil standing over the micro-plane like a giant. He held a silver weapon in his hands that he aimed at the plane, and his cold, emotionless expression said that he wasn't afraid to pull the trigger.

Chapter 13

Time was running out for Micro Dad to stop The Rhino, but he knew it would be too difficult to go against the neutrophil. He had to give up without a fight. Micro Dad stepped out of the micro-plane and was a tiny speck on the road, but he quickly returned to his previous size. The plane fit in the palm of his hand, so he picked it up and placed it into his pocket, hoping to get another chance to use it later. As soon as he turned around, he saw the neutrophil standing several steps away, aiming his weapon directly at him.

The white blood cell was surprisingly tall, about a head taller than Micro Dad. He had a slender build but seemed strong and fit. His face was thin and as spotless as his perfectly white uniform. He wore a humorless and unreadable expression as he stared at Micro Dad with sharp eyes. He could have been mistaken for a statue if he hadn't opened his mouth to speak.

"Stay where you are and put your hands up, germ," he said firmly.

Micro Dad did as he was told. He slowly raised his hands above his head. The neutrophil slowly moved toward him with one hand holding his weapon, then with his other, he reached behind his back and removed a pair of handcuffs. Micro Dad didn't resist as the cell placed them around his wrists as tightly as possible.

"I'd like to see you disappear with these on," said the neutrophil with the same intense, blank expression.

"I wouldn't dream of it," Micro Dad responded warmly and flashed a smile through his mask.

The neutrophil didn't return the smile. He walked behind Micro Dad and shoved him as a sign to start walking. Micro Dad stumbled a little then marched forward. The smile instantly fell from his face.

A large crowd of red blood cells began to gather on the bridge as the white cell led Micro Dad to his awaiting aircraft. They all stared in awe, unsure of what to make of him. He heard whispers as he passed.

"What is it?" a young red cell asked his mother.

"I don't know, sweetie," she responded, "maybe it's some kind of new virus."

"I've never seen anything like it," said another.

After squeezing through the crowd of red cells, Micro Dad and the neutrophil reached the cell's plane. Micro Dad stopped and stared at it, his head tilting back as far as it could go. The plane looked like a large bird. Its wings stretched across the bridge from end to end. During the chase, Micro Dad had thought it was perfectly white, but up close, it was almost clear. Its slender, curved frame was shaped like a boomerang, but it had a sharp, pointed nose like a beak.

"Wow," Micro Dad muttered. "It's like a giant eagle."

"Keep moving," the neutrophil said flatly and gave Micro Dad another hard shove in the back.

Micro Dad was led to the back of the plane, where a long ramp sat on the road. The white blood cell followed him up it, hurrying him along the entire way. Once they entered, the neutrophil escorted Micro Dad into a small square prison cell located in a dark corner of the plane. It was barely big enough for Micro Dad to fit into, but the cell didn't seem to notice or care.

He grabbed Micro Dad by his shoulders and forced him to sit in the lonely chair that was anchored to the floor in the middle of the cage.

"Sit here," the cell grumbled. "It's going to be a while before we get there."

"A while? What's a while?" asked Micro Dad, sounding worried. "Where are we going?"

The neutrophil didn't respond. He just gave Micro Dad a forceful look that spoke for him as if to say, "Don't ask any more questions." Then he turned and exited the cage before slamming the door behind him.

"C'mon," said Micro Dad, "what's the harm in me knowing where I'm going? I'm in handcuffs, remember," he said, raising his arms to show the two metal bracelets.

With that, the neutrophil stopped and glanced over his shoulder at Micro Dad then muttered, "I'm taking you to headquarters. The lymph nodes."

Micro Dad watched the neutrophil walk up a few steps to the plane's cockpit while he sat in the dark cell and thought of a plan to escape. He felt like a T-Rex. His hands were cuffed tightly in front of his body. They were too far apart for him to reach the shrinking button on his wrist. He attempted to reach the micro-plane in his utility belt pocket but couldn't, despite his best efforts. He couldn't bend his arms far enough to reach anything, so he stopped and started to think of a new plan.

The plane started up with a low growl then slowly rolled down the bridge before taking off. It sounded like thunder as it lifted off the ground. It rose high above the road in no time and continued to rise, flying upward at a big angle as if it were crawling up a steep hill. It climbed higher and higher, which was a problem for Micro Dad because he had nothing to hold onto.

He was forced to stand up and slide backward until he crashed into the cage and became pinned against it.

He struggled to speak as he tried to peel himself off the cage. "I bet you think this is so funny, huh!" he shouted.

The neutrophil turned to Micro Dad, and for just a moment, his face softened, and he let a small grin come across his lips. It was the first time the neutrophil had smiled in years, so the grin was awkward and forced. It seemed to take him by surprise because he quickly erased it, and his face turned sour once again.

After the cell's fun, he leveled out the plane. It wasn't often that the cell had fun, but he had had enough for the moment. Micro Dad clumsily staggered back to the chair and sat. He was tired but still confident. He peered up at the neutrophil sitting in the cockpit and started to speak but hesitated for fear of the cell taking him on another rollercoaster ride.

Moments later, he finally got the courage. "Hey. What's your name?"

The neutrophil didn't answer.

"You can't tell me your name?"

The neutrophil cleared his throat as if he would respond but remained silent.

Micro Dad chuckled softly then tried again. "Why am I not surprised? I know you neutrophils are pretty stubborn. That's fine. You don't have to talk. Just listen to me for a second. I'm here to help Alex, okay? I—"

"Quiet!" the neutrophil shouted without even turning to look in Micro Dad's direction. "I hear the same thing from all of you germs every single day. You all say the same thing. You're here to make a better life for yourself or you'll be a productive citizen in the city of Alex, right? You're just like every other germ. You invade then multiply as fast as you can to try to outnumber us.

I've seen it a million times, and it won't happen on my watch."

The plane fell silent. The neutrophil continued to fly while Micro Dad thought of a better approach.

"I'm telling you the truth. I'm here to help whether you like it or not. You have to listen to me. It's important."

To Micro Dad's surprise, the neutrophil bent over the steering wheel and laughed out loud. It was a hardy, spirited laugh, the kind that came straight from the gut. He laughed so hard that Micro Dad thought he was going to burst. Then, just like that, he stopped and sat upright in his seat, returning to perfect posture.

"Yeah, I'm sure it's important. It's always important, germ," he said coldly.

"Look, you may not want to believe anything I say, but it's the truth. I'm here to stop The Rhino."

Suddenly, the neutrophil whipped his head around and stared at Micro Dad. He raised an eyebrow curiously.

"How do you know The Rhino is here? Who told you that?"

Micro Dad exhaled deeply. "That's what I was trying to tell you. I know Alex. I know he's sick."

"So, you're telling me that you know Alex? The Alex? How?"

"I do. He's sick, but he has something really important to do really soon. I'm here to help him get better."

The neutrophil spun around and returned to flying the plane. He stared silently out of the window as if he were deep in thought.

Micro Dad could tell that the wheels were turning in the neutrophil's mind, so he sat quietly and waited for the cell to finish thinking. But after a few minutes, he started to grow impatient.

"So, do you believe me or what?"

The neutrophil still didn't speak, so Micro Dad continued to sit quietly.

"You don't look like any germ I've ever seen," the cell finally said, barely loud enough for Micro Dad to hear. "And Alex being sick is classified. Only white blood cells know about the attack. We didn't want to scare the other cells and cause a panic."

He turned to Micro Dad. He wore a deep frown as he spoke. "I don't know how you found out about it. No other germ would have. So, you might just be telling the truth."

Excitement started to grow inside of Micro Dad. He was sure he was on his way to freedom.

"But you could also be a liar," the neutrophil continued. "Just because I've never seen a germ like you doesn't mean you're not a germ. Maybe you're a new kind of germ. I don't know. My job is to stop every threat from entering the city of Alex. And that's what you are, a threat."

Micro Dad was immediately deflated. He sighed heavily. He had to stay the neutrophil's prisoner after all.

"I can't risk letting you go, and you hurt Alex. I'll let the T cells at headquarters decide what to do with you." Then he pointed out of the window. "We're here."

Headquarters was an enormous building. It was shaped like a dome and was covered with windows as if it were a piece of art on display in the middle of New York City. White planes were scattered throughout the land surrounding it. Some flew off to complete their next mission, racing past the neutrophil's plane and rattling Micro Dad's cage.

Dozens of tiny white dots began to grow larger as the plane approached the dome. They were like a swarm of ants moving across an anthill. As the plane closed in, a huge number of white blood cells came into focus. Micro Dad's heart began to beat faster and harder at the sight of them all. Escaping one white blood cell was hard enough, but he knew escaping hundreds would be nearly impossible.

"There's no way I'm sneaking out of here," he thought.

Headquarters was located in the center of the lymph nodes. Some white cells strolled around casually while others ran laps around the track that circled the building. There were also several groups doing training exercises in the field in the front of headquarters. They performed jumping jacks and push-up routines to stay fit. The cells kept the lymph nodes safe and used it as their command center to fight germs. This made the dome one of the safest and most secure places to be within Alex's body.

The neutrophil headed toward the docking zone and initiated the plane's landing gear and autopilot to begin their decline. He walked down the steps to the cage. Micro Dad lifted his head just as the neutrophil reached it. Their eyes met for a brief moment then the cell opened the door.

"Stand up," he said as he entered and pulled Micro Dad to his feet. "Let's go."

The cell followed Micro Dad to the back of the plane to the exit. He pressed a button and immediately, the door opened, and the ramp began to fall. They waited in silence for it to slowly sink to the ground. The neutrophil was the first to speak. He cleared his throat and attempted to break the tension.

"If you're really here to help Alex then you shouldn't have any trouble convincing the other white blood cells. I'm just doing my job, but I wish you the best of luck."

Micro Dad didn't answer. He was angry, after all. His only reason for being there was to help Alex, but he was being treated like a criminal. But he understood that the neutrophil's job was to keep Alex safe no matter what. Seconds later, he finally spoke.

"Thanks." Then he paused. "I'm Micro Dad, by the way."

The neutrophil quickly turned towards him with a look of total surprise. "I-I'm Phil. Phil Jr.," he managed to say, finding it a little difficult to form a sentence.

"I'm sure that's a pretty common name around here," Micro Dad thought before replying, "Nice to meet you, PJ."

With that, the neutrophil, Phil, grew stiff and his neck snapped toward Micro Dad. He glared intensely at him until, finally, one side of his lip gradually curved upward into half a smile.

"It's Phil."

"Whatever you say, PJ," Micro Dad responded with a grin just as the ramp fell to the ground.

The ramp landed with a light thump. Phil followed Micro Dad as they walked down together. Micro Dad had to steady himself to keep from slipping. If it weren't for Phil, he would have fallen with each step. As they approached the bottom, several pairs of feet covered with white tennis shoes began to appear. They belonged to dozens of white blood cells, who all gathered around Phil's plane just to get a good look at the strange germ that had caused so much panic in the vein on the way to the lungs.

Once the two made it all the way down the ramp, Micro Dad saw just how many white cells had gathered. They were scattered in all directions, too many for him to count. He expected to hear a lot of noise with so many cells huddled together, but there was only silence, not even a breath or whisper. Micro Dad stepped down and shuffled nervously past the first few cells and finally caused the stir he had been expecting.

"Is that him?" someone in the crowd whispered.

"No, couldn't be. Too tall," someone else answered.

"Smaller than I thought," said a cell in the back.

"He doesn't look like any germ I've ever seen before," said another. "Must be from another country."

Traveling from the plane to the front door of headquarters required them to walk down one long, straight road, which made the trip seem longer but even more so to Micro Dad because he was gawked at the entire way. Whispers grew louder and became jumbled conversations that Micro Dad couldn't quite make out. Every pair of eyes stayed locked on him as he moved through the crowd. They followed each step he took as if he were a magician in the middle of a trick that no one wanted to miss.

Phil and Micro Dad finally reached the building then hiked dozens of steps leading up the steep stairway. They eventually led to a huge set of glass doors with a dark iron frame. Once they entered headquarters, Micro Dad instantly heard endless ringing from phones in the lobby. An office assistant, who wore cat-eyed glasses and incredibly bright red lipstick, sat perched in a chair behind a desk and juggled the phones. She answered each call with, "City of Alex Precinct Twenty-one. Please hold," then immediately proceeded to hang up.

She didn't seem to notice Micro Dad and Phil making their way through the grand hall or the large crowd that stared at them through the windows from the outside. Micro Dad couldn't help but gaze straight up in amazement at the station's enormous crystal-clear roof as he walked. Every object in the building seemed to absorb the light that reflected from it, making each one shine as if it were made of diamonds.

The large room was practically empty except for a few white cells that walked hurriedly across the lobby and out of the double doors. They passed the remaining crowd of cells without noticing them. Micro Dad was relieved that no one followed them inside, but he still felt like an animal in a zoo as they stared at him through several windows.

The polished lobby floors led to an elevator that sat open and ready for them to use. Phil led Micro Dad inside then pressed the last button on the board for the fiftieth floor. It lit up, the doors closed, then the elevator began to rise. The ride was strangely relaxing for Micro Dad. His mission had been thrilling up to that point, so he enjoyed the rare moment of peace, but the ride quickly ended, and the doors opened to chaos.

Phones rang relentlessly, even more than the lobby. There were too many white blood cells to count. They were holding the phones to their ears and yelling back into them. Micro Dad tried to hear what they were yelling about but couldn't. He thought he heard a cell say, "Don't worry, ma'am, the germ has been arrested. Everyone is safe."

Phil left Micro Dad by the elevator and walked over to a few of the cells and asked, "Have you seen Chief T?"

But no one could hear him. They were all too busy answering phones and arguing with one another, so Phil went back to Micro Dad and began leading him through the middle of the room toward an office that sat strangely in the center. Without warning, a loud shout rose above everyone, silencing them all.

"Be quiet!" screamed the voice. Even the phones were seemingly intimidated and immediately stopped ringing. Then the sound of hard footsteps marching across the floor echoed through the office, followed by the sound of a screeching door opening.

Suddenly, an incredibly large white blood cell appeared in the doorway. His muscles bulged out of his tight-fitting shirt, putting his massive arms and chest on display. He was so tall that he had to lower his head to avoid hitting the doorframe as he stepped out of the office. Other white cells parted for him as he walked, allowing Micro Dad to see just how cartoonishly uneven his body was. His huge upper body rested on a pair of scrawny legs like a piece of steak attached to a pair of pencils.

"Is this him?" the large cell barked, pointing as he marched straight toward Micro Dad. "Is this the germ that caused so much destruction on the bridge today?"

For a moment, Micro Dad thought the cell would walk right through him, but he quickly stopped right in front of him and Phil. He was a full head taller than Micro Dad, so his shoulders hunched forward as he stopped speaking to stare down at them both. His face had a look that said the cell was permanently angry. His jaw was clenched, his nose flared out wide and blew big gusts of air down to a hairy mustache that lay across his upper lip.

He eventually loosened his jaw and asked again, "Was that you?"

Micro Dad bent his neck back so that he could stare up at the cell. "Well, actu—"

"I wasn't really asking you the question, germ. I know it was you!" he shouted and stamped his foot like a pouting toddler. "I know it was you because you were caught by one of this city's best white cells."

He glanced over at Phil and gave him a quick nod of approval. "Nice job, son."

"Just doing my job, Chief T," Phil said blankly, his back stiff and eyes focused straight ahead.

"Nice to meet you, Chief T. I'm—" Micro Dad started to say but was cut short.

"Why do you keep talking?" Chief T asked casually. "You can't talk your way out of this. There's no telling how long it's going to take to clean up that mess you made on the bridge. You caused panic and damage to government property when you flew over the vein. Countless red cells were taken to the hospital and even more are out of a job now because their cars were destroyed. How can you explain that?"

The white blood cells in the office all remained soundless and motionless, their ears raised, waiting for Micro Dad to reply.

He stood silent for a brief moment, deciding if Chief T was actually waiting for an answer, then decided to speak. "I can't explain that," he said. "I'm sorry for scaring the red cells, but I didn't destroy any of their cars. That was the neutrophils. I didn't mean for anyone to get hurt, but I'm here to help Alex."

Chief T scoffed. "You're here to help Alex? You? You're a germ. There's nothing you can do except leave the city of Alex and go back to whatever trashcan or sewer you crawled out of."

Micro Dad was usually able to smile through insults, but Chief T's words made him furious. His jaw tightened. He took a step toward the chief until the handcuffs on his outstretched arms bumped the large cell in the stomach. He was too close to look up into the cell's eyes, so Micro Dad just spoke to his chest.

His eyes narrowed and he said, "I know you're the chief, and I don't want to interfere with your work, but I made a promise that I would do everything I could to help Alex. I fixed his throat and sinuses this morning, all while you were probably sitting in your office squeezing into that shirt."

A few white cells giggled in the back of the room. Micro Dad took a few steps back and hesitated for only a second before continuing, "I'm Micro Dad. Nice to meet you."

Voices suddenly sprang up throughout the office. Micro Dad

stood tall and even poked his chest out a little after speaking. There was no doubt in his mind he would be set free immediately. After all, he had saved Alex from bacteria and viruses many times throughout the years. He didn't want to brag, but he was a hero.

But to his surprise, the room exploded into laughter. Even neutrophils that never usually showed any emotion toppled over their desks. Almost every cell in the room had tears streaming down theirs faces and were grabbing their sides from laughing pain, including Chief T, who had fallen on the floor next to Micro Dad's feet.

Only Micro Dad and Phil stayed quiet and waited for the cells to stop. It took several minutes. Then every blood cell in the room stood to attention once again as if nothing had happened. Chief T pulled himself up using Micro Dad's legs for support and stood rigidly before speaking.

"You can't be serious?" he sighed. "Micro Dad is a myth. Cells have been telling stories of him for generations, but they're just stories."

Micro Dad interrupted. "Hold on a second. All of you think I'm just a story? I'm Micro Dad. I fought bronchitis just a few years ago. You really think I'm just a story?"

He had to remember that white cells normally lived short lives of only a few months. They grew from babies to adults in a matter of days. So to them, the last time he was there would have felt like hundreds of years instead of just a few. It was no surprise that his existence had become a fairytale.

Chief T continued, "Where'd you hear the story, huh? At one of your filthy germ bars? And you thought you could come here and pretend to be Micro Dad?" The chief chuckled. "You're worse than I thought. Get him outta here. Take him to the nose for a snot removal."

A group of neutrophil guards dressed in white suits immediately approached Micro Dad from all sides. They moved in closer with their arms raised, ready to grab him, but before they could seize him, he yelled, "Wait. I know about The Rhino!"

The guards stopped in their tracks then looked over at Chief T. Their eyes bulged from their heads with shock.

"That's classified!" the Chief shouted. "How do you know about that? Are you working with that virus?"

"I know because I'm Alex's dad and because I want to help him feel better. The science fair means a lot to him, but he has a cold. The Rhino is here destroying everything. I saw the damage that was done to his throat and sinuses, so I helped fix them like I told you earlier. I'm not here to step on your toes, Chief. I'm just here to help."

He glanced around the room and became more hopeful. Many of the white cells' faces started to soften and murmurs washed across the room, sounding promising. The cells all turned toward Chief T and waited for his response.

The chief stared at Micro Dad curiously. He seemed to be deep in thought, but he quickly destroyed all of Micro Dad's hope.

"Let me stop you right there," he said coldly. "I don't care who you say you are or what you say you want to accomplish. You can't just come here and expect me to believe you're a superhero and think I'm going to let you do whatever you want. That's not how this works."

Micro Dad felt his jaw tighten once again.

"I've been the chief of police for Precinct twenty-one for three long months." Chief T continued, "I've heard every story in the book. You germs will say anything to come here and take over."

His arms waved as he shouted. He began to pace between two desks, waving his arms as he spoke. "I come from a long line of T cells who were on the police force before me, and they fought the worst of the worst, so I know what I'm doing. We don't want or need the help of some germ."

With that, Chief T nodded to the guards standing beside Micro Dad. "Get him outta here."

"Chief, may I say—" Phil blurted out, shocking everyone, including himself.

"No, you may not, Captain," Chief T instantly interrupted. "Now, take him to extraction."

This time, the guards hesitated. They looked at each other and waited for one of the others to make the first move. They glanced over at the chief then back at Micro Dad, unsure of what to do. Micro Dad's eyes darted back and forth between them.

Chief T grew angrier each second the guards refused to follow his orders. His cheeks turned from white to a rosy pink then to a crimson red. He was a volcano ready to explode. Every cell in the room anxiously waited to see what would happen next, but Phil was the first to break the tension.

"Chief," he said then stepped forward to stand beside Micro Dad. "I saw what happened on the bridge today, and what he did was unbelievable. I've never seen a germ disappear in the blink of an eye like that." Then he moved in front of the chief. "I've only heard of such incredible things in stories. Stories you used to tell me, Dad."

Excitement and barely audible whispers spread to each of the cells.

"This is like a novella," a cell exclaimed from all the way in the back of the room next to the water cooler. He was answered with a loud shush from the others.

Phil continued, "We've all heard stories of the legendary Micro Dad. You and I both used to believe in him, and here he is, standing in front of us. We'd be crazy not to accept his help. What do you say, Chief?"

Chief T turned as red as a strawberry. His nose flared again, breathing hard enough to blow the candles out on a birthday cake. He had his fists clenched tightly, falling beside his bony thighs. Phil didn't back down. He stood his ground and waited for the outcome.

The chief raised his huge right arm and threw it towards him. Micro Dad flinched, expecting the chief's massive fist to connect with any part of Phil's body that would leave a bruise, but the blow never came. Instead, Chief T reached out to Phil with his palm open and his fingers spread to shake Phil's hand.

Everyone was shocked, including Phil, who hesitated before taking it. When he finally did, Chief T's enormous hand swallowed his as he looked down on Phil and grinned slightly before speaking.

"A good chief of police should always follow good advice, even if it isn't their own. Remember that when it's your time to be chief."

His color returned to its normal soft white within moments, then he turned to Micro Dad.

"What's your plan?"

Chapter 14

Everyone, including Micro Dad, was so wrapped up in watching Chief T and Phil that no one heard the elevator beep or the scraping metal sound when the doors slid open. A figure wearing a dark hooded robe over its entire body walked out slowly. The robe was too large to reveal anything about the figure, but as it moved, a bit of a sharp white tip peeked out from underneath the hood. The figure crept to the right toward a large window that had a great view of the rest of the lymph nodes.

Once it reached it, the hood that blanketed the figure suddenly began to shake. The disguise quivered from underneath for a few moments before four spheres appeared out of the robe's long sleeves. They were clear orbs that contained a shadow of grey smoke that seemed to dance inside each one as if it wanted its freedom. They moved like thunderstorm clouds trapped in a bottle.

The robe gradually folded as the figure bowed to place the spheres on the floor at the bottom of the window frame. In a hurry, it shuffled back to the awaiting elevator in short but quick strides then pressed the button labeled "Garage". The round button lit up, but nothing happened. Even the small squares that sat above the door refused to shine.

A minute passed with no sign of life from the elevator. The robe began to tremble as the figure became more agitated. Its hood moved further backward as it stared straight at the spheres that still sat below the window across the room then back up at the squares again and again. The robe shook with more force as the sound of heavy boots banging against a hard floor echoed throughout the quiet office.

The loud thump of the figure's foot tapping the elevator floor quickly increased. Before long, the sound became less of a tap and more of a hard stomp to the ground. It was as if each loud clunk would force the elevator to work. Miraculously, after one last attempt the elevator suddenly sprang to life. A button with an arrow pointing down flickered then brightened as a robotic voice rumbled out of the elevator's speaker.

"Going down," it proclaimed.

Most white cells were still listening to Micro Dad discussing the plan to beat The Rhino, but over a dozen were on the edge of the crowd and heard the announcement. They turned to see the hooded figure tapping its foot wildly. It was waiting for the elevator doors to close. Unfortunately, they refused to move at all.

The cells were immediately suspicious. They whispered to each other then carefully approached the elevator, forming a line as they crept forward. They were only steps away from it when one cell shouted out.

"Hey, you inside the elevator, stop what you're doing, take off the hood and put your hands up."

The tapping quickly ended, and the figure froze. The conversation between Chief T, Phil and Micro Dad suddenly stopped at the sound of the shout. Everyone instantly looked over at the group of cells moving toward the intruder, who didn't move an inch. Even the robe turned stiff.

Seconds ticked away before the figure finally made a move. It faced them but showed nothing but a dark shadow behind the hood. It slowly brought its long sleeves up to the top of its head and pulled back the hood, revealing The Rhino. A wide, joyous grin stretched across his face as if he had just won a game that only he was playing.

Gasps erupted throughout the office. The wall of cells immediately grabbed their weapons from their holsters and aimed them at the virus, whose smirk instantly turned to wild laughter at seeing the weapons pointed in his direction. His laughter filled the office. Cells quickly panicked at the sound and drew their weapons and ran to the elevator. Soon, there was a swarm of white cells gathered around him.

Confusion followed. White cells shouted over one another and scrambled to get a closer look at The Rhino or to avoid him altogether. Every cell was afraid of getting too close for fear of being touched and turned into one of his copies.

Micro Dad gazed over the cells' shoulders and saw glimpses of the virus. He attempted to squeeze through the large crowd that surrounded him but couldn't get through. They were all too closely packed together and blocked his path.

The Rhino continued laughing as he watched the chaos unfold. Every one of his crooked yellow teeth was exposed. The white cells shouted orders at him, but he ignored them all.

Some shouted, "Don't move!"

Others yelled, "Get down on the ground!"

The Rhino did neither. He shuffled backward until his back crashed into the elevator wall then stood in silence and waited. His eyes never met any of the white cells. They stayed locked on the four spheres that sat on the other side of the room.

In an instant, light puffs of smoke appeared out of each of them as if four small fires had been lit. The breaths of smoke twisted and curved, becoming one. It floated through the air and slowly disappeared into the window above it. Then all at once, the shells broke, scattering uneven lines across the spheres until they all looked like cracked eggs.

Immediately, a storm of dark grey smoke poured out of each one until it formed one large cloud that suddenly attached itself to the window, swallowing everything it touched. A massive hole soon emerged and stretched out along the walls, consuming every bit of it. It finally stopped just before reaching the wall's corners, but it showed no signs of disappearing. Instead, the center of the cloud began to rotate like a spinning top. Its size grew with its speed until every inch of it began to swirl like the eye of a hurricane.

The core became a black hole. Once its transformation was complete, the hole began to suck up objects around the office and spit them out of the building. It started with pens, pencils, and paper. They were ripped off desks and thrown into the air before being carried into the large vortex and flung out into the crowd of unsuspecting white blood cells below.

Chairs scraped across the floor then flew into the air and into the cloud's mouth. They immediately came out the other side, falling towards planes on the runway that prepared to take off. Many bystanders on the ground avoided injury by sprinting for cover but were nearly struck by the flying office supplies. The white cells in the heart of the storm on the fiftieth floor weren't so lucky, however.

The cells hid behind large desks when the storm began. Many dove to the floor and crawled toward the heaviest objects they could find. They held onto them as tightly as they could, dropping their weapons in the process.

The cells that surrounded The Rhino ran for cover to save their own lives. The Rhino, on the other hand, remained calm and relaxed as he crouched low at the back of the elevator. He kept his arms outstretched and held onto the rail that was secured to the wall. Surprisingly, as the winds picked up speed, the elevator decided to escape. It came back to life, and The Rhino's smile, like a box of broken yellow crayons, was brighter than ever as he watched his weapon lay waste to the white blood cells' headquarters until the doors closed completely, then he was gone.

Micro Dad held the knobs of a large filing cabinet while he drifted in the wind like a swaying flag. Chief T and Phil hunkered down behind a desk that slowly crept toward the swirling vortex. The wind tugged on Micro Dad's legs, but he held on with all his strength. He tried to walk his hands to other objects to crouch down beside Phil, but the handcuffs around his wrists left him trapped. The chains clattered and banged against the old copper cabinet like a dinner bell for the black hole. Micro Dad's grip weakened with every passing moment.

He turned his head and shouted at Phil, hoping to be heard over the sound of the whistling wind, "Get me out of these handcuffs. I can stop this thing!"

The words traveled through the heavy storm and reached Phil's ears. His head shot up at the sound of Micro Dad's voice. He glanced over and saw Micro Dad being violently pulled by the savage gusts, then his face hardened. He knew there was only one thing he could do. He took a deep breath and prepared to leap to the cabinet.

He stuck his head out from behind the desk just enough to check if the coast was clear. Without warning, a chair flew over his head, nearly crashing into him. At the last second, Chief T grabbed Phil's collar and pulled him back just in time.

"Thanks," Phil said behind heavy breaths.

"Don't mention it," Chief T said casually, his eyes filled with worry. "Are you sure you know what you're doing?"

"No, but I have to take the chance to protect Alex, right?" Then Phil turned and dove forward, soaring right over a passing table and straight to the cabinet.

He attempted to grab every object in sight before finally landing on a handle three drawers to the right of Micro Dad. Every muscle in his arms tightened as he pulled as hard as he could to press himself against the cold piece of furniture. Once his upper body rested on the cabinet, Phil tucked his legs in then grabbed the closest handles to him and climbed until he reached Micro Dad.

Carefully, Phil released his right hand and reached into his pocket to remove a tiny silver key. His fingers tightened around it, afraid he would drop it and it would get inhaled by the grey clouds. He grabbed Micro Dad's wrist, leaned over and yelled above the loud swooshing of the wind.

"You ready?"

"About as ready as I can be," Micro Dad said with a look that showed the amount of pain he was in.

Phil quickly unlocked both bracelets from his wrists. They fell toward the ground but were instantly caught by the wind and swallowed up by the hole. Without delay, Micro Dad removed a round white bead from his utility belt. It was like a small pearl.

He gently twisted it back and forth between his left thumb and middle finger, slowly and carefully, as if he were tuning an instrument. After a few seconds, the bead began to change. It went from a pale white to a dim blue, then to a gleaming purple that poured light onto Micro Dad's hand.

As he held the tiny ball of light, the swirling black hole continued to eat. More and more desks and chairs disappeared and left many of the white cells exposed and clawing at the floor to keep from being lifted away. Several T cells formed chains, holding on to each other's arms while others wrapped their arms around anything that was bolted to the ground.

The bead vibrated as light rushed out of it. Micro Dad held on firmly, waiting for the right moment. His fingers clamped around the cabinet's handle. They became weaker and weaker. One by one, they loosened until he held on with nothing but his thumb and index finger.

Finally, even those had had enough. They gave up and went limp, falling from the handle. Phil dove forward and tried to catch Micro Dad's hand, but it was too late. Micro Dad was pulled through the air like a thin sheet of paper.

The wind carried him underneath a nearby table, past a group of white cells that crouched low and scratched the ground with every bit of their strength, straight toward the awaiting black hole. The vortex seemed to smile and open wider when it saw Micro Dad sailing towards it, as if he would be its main dish. Micro Dad held the glowing purple bead tightly until he was in the middle of the room, halfway to the eye of the storm. He casually opened his hand and let go of the tiny, shining ball.

It floated like a speck of dust, swirling across the room in small loops before flying into the vortex. But instead of being launched out into the open air, the bead seemed to stick to the spiraling cloud. Then in an instant, a flash of purple light exploded from the cloud, covering the black hole completely.

For a single moment, the entire room was nothing but purple light. The flash was blinding. Every cell had to shut its eyes to protect them from the intense burst. Seconds later when they opened them, not only were they all safe on the ground, but the black hole had disappeared.

Only a large empty space remained where the office wall once stood. The wind had stopped rustling and plucking furniture from the office and tossing it out into the open air. The room had fallen completely silent. Nothing was left of headquarters except for a few large desks that had slid to the center of the room and three old cabinets that the cells clung to.

The stunned white blood cells all released their hands from one another's and walked around the empty office freely. Most were unharmed, but some had a few bumps and bruises from flying debris. Micro Dad, who had collapsed in front of the vortex just as the light exploded out of the bead, slowly picked himself up. His armor had some slight damage from the hard fall, but he was untouched.

He glanced down at the floor and had to squint to make out the dark grey vortex resting at his feet. It was tiny, but it continued to spin, completely unaware that it had been shrunken down to the size of Micro Dad's fingernail. Suddenly, in the blink of an eye, it disappeared. The bead had worked perfectly, shrinking the black hole out of existence.

Micro Dad forced a small grin on his lips as he walked to the large hole in the wall and looked out over the edge in shock. Nothing stood between him and the open air of the lymph node. He could clearly see what looked like miles into the distance. Broken planes, chairs, and desks were littered throughout the ground below. White cells began appearing from inside the building and looked up, waiting to see if more objects would rain down on them.

He continued to brood until Phil approached him and broke his concentration.

"You saved our lives," he said then paused, not knowing what else to say to show his gratitude but remain tough at the same time. "Thanks," was all he could think to say.

"Don't mention it," Micro Dad quickly answered, knowing

how awkward the white cell must have felt, but he continued to stare at the damage to the lymph nodes.

Seconds passed before he spoke again. "Do you have any leads on where The Rhino could be hiding? I'm running out of time," he said flatly.

Phil let out a deep sigh before speaking. "Well, not exactly," he said through clenched teeth as if it hurt him just to form the sentence. "We haven't had much luck and haven't been able to track him after each of his attacks. He and his copies hit their targets then vanish."

He turned to look around the room, his eyes narrowing. "He's good at hiding. Our best cells have been on the hunt for days, but all we've ever run into are copies, and they never give him up when we interrogate them." Phil hesitated for a moment before continuing. "Today was the first time any of us have even seen the real Rhino. We were this close to capturing him!" he held out his index finger and thumb and moved them close together to emphasize his point. "I should have been the one to arrest him."

Micro Dad, seeing Phil's frustration, turned to him. "We'll get him," he said with enough confidence to make Phil believe it. "He has to be hiding somewhere in the lungs. We need to put out a bulletin asking every cell in the area to help find The Rhino."

"That would cause every good citizen of Alex to panic!" Chief T shouted from across the room then marched toward Micro Dad, his heavy boots pounding the ground loudly. "This was a small setback, but believe me, we have everything under control. We don't need to involve civilians."

"But that actually doesn't sound like a bad idea, Chief. It could save us a lot of time," said Phil.

"You think so, Captain? Well, you aren't old enough to

remember the chickenpox scare. Cells nearly started a riot when they thought that virus was on the loose. I'm saying no, and that's the end of it."

"Chief," Micro Dad interrupted, "I thought we had an agreement. You said you were willing to let me help track down The Rhino."

"I did say that. And I meant it. You can help, but I'm still the chief, and I don't want any civilians knowing that cold virus is running around the city of Alex. Are we clear?"

Micro Dad and Phil both nodded their heads reluctantly.

"You're probably right about The Rhino hiding in the lungs," Chief T continued, "but after what just happened here, it's important for the lymph nodes to be healthy, so we have to fix headquarters. But I don't have enough spare cells to search for The Rhino and rebuild HQ, so it will have to be a secret mission with a small team."

Chief T looked around the room and shouted, "I'll need a volunteer to escort Micro Dad to the lungs and find The Rhino."

Surprisingly, no one moved an inch. They all stared blankly at Chief T without saying a word. The cells were either too nervous to work with Micro Dad or just too starstruck. A few had looks of horror from The Rhino's attack and still couldn't speak. Phil was the only one to step forward. He approached Micro Dad and jingled a pair of keys.

"I'll drive."

Chapter 15

Alex sat on his dresser and stared at the walkie-talkie in his hand. He had called Micro Dad again and again countless times. He was waiting for a sign that everything was all right. His nose and throat felt great, but he was still exhausted and felt sick.

He attempted to call Micro Dad for the thousandth time, but again, he got no response. So, he messaged his friends to let them know he wasn't missing the science fair, to which Josh replied back with a picture of a thumbs up and Aiden with a video of a baby excitedly dancing in its diaper. Soon after, Alex finally decided to call his mom, Camille, who had sent at least fifteen messages to check on him and his dad because they both had not responded. He responded with an exaggerated yawn and explained that he had been resting like she had asked him to, and that Frank had gone to the grocery store and must have forgotten his phone.

Camille didn't buy it. Her mom instincts started to tingle, telling her that he was hiding something. She could always tell, but before she could question him, a client walked in, so she had to cut the conversation short. She blew two kisses into the phone then was gone.

Alex had nothing else to do but sit and stare at the walkie as if he were going to force Micro Dad to speak on the other end. He sat without moving a muscle until, surprisingly, the left side of his neck began to itch and quickly became irritated. He used two fingers to rub the spot, thinking it was just a growing pimple, but it was a round pea-sized ball underneath his skin. It was extremely sensitive and throbbing uncontrollably.

Alex grabbed his phone and quickly found his favorite online medical website. He typed "pea-sized ball in neck" in the search bar then scrolled through the list of options. There were several pages that gave detailed descriptions about how the lymph nodes swell in a person's neck due to infections caused by viruses like the rhinovirus. He read each line quickly but carefully, taking note of how germs attack them.

Once he finished the article, he exited out of the site then thought, "Micro Dad has to have somethin' to do with this." Then he held the walkie-talkie up to his mouth and called once again.

Chapter 16

Micro Dad rode next to Phil inside the small cockpit of the cell's plane. He twisted and squirmed from side to side just to fit comfortably, while Phil sat perfectly still without seeming to notice Micro Dad's movement. The cell kept his eyes straight ahead, flying with the intense focus of a hawk, ignoring all distractions, including his passenger. Finally giving up, Micro Dad found the best position and sat with his hands folded into his lap.

"I usually fly alone, by the way," Phil said without turning to look in Micro Dad's direction. "That's why it's a little tight in here."

Micro Dad quickly responded, "It's fine. I hadn't noticed," and waved his hand casually as if he had plenty of space and wasn't in danger of folding into a pretzel. Then he rotated and turned to Phil.

"So, the chief's your dad, huh? That must be—" he paused to think of the right word before finally choosing, "*interesting*."

"What do you mean by that?" asked Phil.

"Nothing. I just mean he's a pretty big cell and has a pretty big personality to match. So, it must have been interesting growing up with him."

Phil nodded, understanding Micro Dad's point. "We don't like to talk about it while we're at work. We don't want anyone to think he's giving me special treatment just because I'm his son. I became captain on my own without his help. Chief has done a lot of great things for the city of Alex and is a hero to a lot of cells here, so I don't want to be treated differently by the others. And he's not always like that. He's usually quiet at home." Phil laughed. "He even goes to the senior cell center where the older white and red blood cells live to visit them once a week."

"I guess you can't judge a book by its cover," Micro Dad said with a smile then fell silent.

It only lasted for a moment. "What's Alex like?" Phil asked, trying to hold in his excitement.

Micro Dad flashed a wide grin. "He's really smart and creative. And fun. He still likes hanging out with me sometimes, which is pretty cool. We talk all the time. I was telling him about my mission before I met you, actually," he said, smiling even wider, but the more he thought about Alex, the smaller his smile became.

He fell forward and got to his feet, crouching low to avoid hitting the ceiling, then he quickly took the walkie out of his utility belt. "I forgot about Alex," he muttered then fumbled to talk into it. "Alex. Come in, Alex. Over."

"You're calling Alex now? Like right now? Seriously?" Phil stammered, taking his eyes away from flying to stare at Micro Dad with a stunned expression. Then he immediately turned back to stare out of the plane's window. His hands began to tremble while holding on to the steering wheel.

"Should I say something to him? No. That would be weird, right? No. It'll be fine, right? No," Phil said to no one in particular.

Micro Dad looked over at him with a sideways glance. "Are you goin' to be okay?"

Phil, realizing he had said everything out loud, quickly stopped talking and continued flying. "I'm fine," he nearly shouted then bit his bottom lip to keep from panicking any more.

"Good," said Micro Dad then repeated, "Alex. Come in, Alex. Over."

Seconds later, Alex's voice came through the walkie in a huff. He was panting hard as if he had just finished running a mile. "Micro Dad! What happened? Where have you been?" he asked between gasps.

"Hey, Al. It's a long story. I'll fill you in later. Why are you breathing so hard?"

"I was in the bathroom. I hadn't brushed my teeth today. And I can't go to school with my breath smelling like I've been eating out of the dumpster. But I didn't realize that I left the walkie in my room, so I had to hurry and finish then run back. Where are you?"

"I'm on my way to the lungs. Al—"

Alex interrupted, "I thought you were already going to the lungs. What happened?"

"I almost made it but got a little sidetracked," he answered, his voice trailing off as he glanced over at Phil, who was using one hand to steer and biting the nails on the other. "How ya feelin'?"

"A lot better, but my throat hurts again. I have a small lump under my chin. It's a swollen lymph node, right?" Alex asked, already sure of the answer.

Micro Dad balled up a fist, thinking about The Rhino nearly destroying headquarters. "Yeah, Al," he sighed, "you're right. The Rhino attacked headquarters on that lymph node and wrecked it pretty bad. That's why it's painful for you right now."

"I knew it. Did you beat him?"

Micro Dad sighed. "Nope. He got away. That's why we're going back to the lungs to catch him."

"We?" Alex asked. "Who are you with?"

Micro Dad glanced back over at Phil and smirked. "I'm with one of your white blood cells. One of your best, actually. His name's PJ."

Phil snapped his head to glare at Micro Dad, his eyes bulging. "It's Phil," he said in a harsh tone covered by a whisper.

"Really?" Alex sounded surprised, "You're really with one of my white blood cells right now? You serious?"

"Yeah, I'm serious. Listen to this." Micro Dad stuck the walkie out to Phil and whispered, "Talk to him."

Phil immediately froze. His body tightened. The fear swelling inside him was completely new. His hand gripped the steering wheel even tighter, nearly crushing it.

"Say something," Micro Dad repeated and pointed to the walkie.

Phil cleared his throat then began to stammer uncontrollably. "H-H-Hi. Hi." He looked around the cockpit as if he were looking for the words to throw together to make a good sentence. "I-I am. I'm Phil. I, uh, I'm a captain. I'm a white blood cell. Well, you have a lot of different white blood cells. But I'm one. I'm a neutrophil. We, uh, well, we do a lot. I don't want to bore you with that stuff. This isn't a classroom. I'm not a teacher. Unless you want to learn. Not saying you don't already know. You probably already know. You're a smart kid. Not that I'm calling you a kid. Well, I know you're growing up and not really a kid any more. I kind of watched you grow up. That sounded weird. Sorry, uh, I-I'm rambling. It's an honor to meet you, sir." Phil finished the long-winded speech with a bow toward the walkie-talkie then slumped into his chair and patted the top of his head while mouthing, "Why would you say that?" to the steering wheel.

Alex exclaimed, "Wow! This is so cool. I'm actually talking to a white blood cell. How awesome is that! No one would ever believe this."

Phil quickly raised his head and gave a huge smile.

"You're helping my dad beat The Rhino?"

"Yes, sir!" Phil said with more confidence and a slightly deeper voice than his own, "and we will beat him, sir. I'll stop at nothing to help you get to the science fair."

"You have some strong white blood cells, Al," said Micro Dad. "We're definitely going to stop him. So just hang tight for a little while longer. Can you do that?"

Alex gave a deep breath then answered, "Roger that, Micro Dad. I'll keep waiting. Let me know if I can help. I'd really like to help."

Micro Dad chuckled. "Roger that, Al. Over and out."

"It was nice to meet you, PJ. Over and out."

Phil's smile stretched across his face. "Good luck at the science fair, sir. Over and out!" he shouted back just before the walkie clicked off.

Chapter 17

Phil rambled ceaselessly the rest of the way to the lungs. A smile was draped across his mouth.

"Alex called me PJ. PJ. I guess it has a nice ring to it. I can't believe I actually talked to Alex. The Alex. This is amazing. I knew it was going to be a good day today when I woke up this morning. I could feel it in my plasma."

Micro Dad tried to get a word in, but Phil rambled on and on without taking a breath. All he could do was look through the window out into the vein. The traffic was lighter and smoother than before, but cars continued to beep at each other out of habit. Their horns sounded like muffled chirps below the soaring plane.

Soon after, they approached the entrance to the lungs. Micro Dad could hardly recognize the street he had just seen not long before. The entire road was spotless and looked newly paved. The walls of the bridge were fixed. There were no destroyed cars or wreckage from the white cells' planes scattered from end to end.

Phil flew past without noticing. His chatter only ended when the pair reached the large gate. A security checkpoint inspected the ID of every individual waiting to enter, deciding whether or not to let them go or take them for questioning or removal. But Phil and Micro Dad flew right over the border and into the lungs without anyone stopping them. Phil lifted his hand to his head in a salute as they drifted by.

Once they entered into the lungs, an enormous city quickly

came into view. It was full of identical factories as large as stadiums. Each one stood side by side along the highway. They were all made with rusty brick that lit up their path.

Traffic disappeared completely once the red blood cells drove into the lungs. The highway instantly split into hundreds of narrow roads, each one leading to a giant factory. Once the cells reached one, they parked their cars and trucks and waited while workers quickly unloaded large barrels marked "CO2" then tossed them into a bin marked "waste" with a recycling symbol displayed on the front. When the barrels were all unloaded, the workers loaded the vehicles full of silver containers marked "oxygen" then led the red blood cells back out of the factory and away from the lungs to deliver the containers to other parts of the body. The workers' speed could have challenged the best pit crew in NASCAR. It took less than a second for the cells to enter the factory, unload and reload, then race off once again.

The red cells moved in and out of the buildings as if the hundreds of factories were part of one huge assembly line. Cars entered and exited the factories at the exact same time in perfect harmony without missing a beat. Micro Dad stared out of his window at the rhythmic routine, completely hypnotized.

Phil didn't even notice the traveling red blood cells. He raced past the buildings in a hurry, his eyes scanning everything around him, looking for anything different from the steady rhythm of the red blood cells entering and exiting the factories. He was once again the hawk stalking the ground below him.

He clearly knew his way around the lungs. He dodged each building effortlessly as if they weren't even there. Micro Dad held on tight to the bottom of his seat but enjoyed the ride, other than when he nearly fainted when Phil dove straight down to the street to get a better look at the driver of a slow-moving rust-colored pickup truck, thinking it could be The Rhino, and almost ran right into the tail end of it. He groaned when it turned out just to be an old, grey-haired red cell. So he quickly rose high into the sky once again, but not before Micro Dad could get a good look at the cell's bumper sticker that read, "How am I driving? Call 1-800-I'm-old-and-don't-care."

Micro Dad chuckled and turned to Phil. "So, what's the plan? Should we keep flying around looking for old, slow-driving cells?"

Phil, no longer in a laughing mood, stared out at the buildings below and spoke softly. "The Rhino is around here somewhere. I know it. All he has to do is make one mistake and I'll catch him. Just wait and see."

Not knowing what else to say, Micro Dad just nodded his head and tapped his knees with his fingers. After a few seconds of silence, he thought of an idea. "Maybe we should split up," he said aloud. "That way we can cover more ground. I have my micro-plane right here in my pocket. You can let me out and I'll just—"

"Remember what Chief T said," Phil interrupted. "I'm not supposed to let you out of my sight."

"I don't see Chief T around here. Do you? How's he going to know?"

"The chief gave me an order, so I intend on following it," Phil said with a heavy sigh.

"But you said that we have to start taking some risks to help Alex, right? I'm not asking you to disobey orders. Just make the right choice," Micro Dad said then stood up to leave. "We're running out of time and not getting any closer to finding The Rhino this way."

Phil lunged forward and pressed an orange button to engage autopilot, then leapt in front of Micro Dad, blocking the stairs and the only way out of the cockpit. "I can't let you do that," he said firmly, his fists resting beside his legs but balled up tight.

The two stood face-to-face and stared at each other with piercing eyes, neither one willing to move an inch. They didn't even blink for fear of missing a fist flying toward them in that half a second it would take for their eyelids to close then reopen. The tension in the cockpit was thick and seemed to make the room much smaller. With no end to the standoff in sight, it was Micro Dad who finally spoke.

"We can't do this all day, PJ. Alex needs us. The both of us," he said as he relaxed and ended his intense stare. "I'm here to help, but I'm your guest, so I'll follow your lead. Is that cool?" Micro Dad reached out for a handshake.

Phil stood perfectly still for another second, just in case Micro Dad was planning a sneak attack. When nothing happened, he relaxed, loosened his balled-up fist, and stuck out his hand to shake. But just before taking Micro Dad's hand, he saw something out the plane's window ahead of them. A smile quickly grew on his face as he rushed past Micro Dad, almost knocking him over. He jumped into his seat, disengaged autopilot, and continued to fly.

"You neutrophils really aren't the most friendly, are you?" asked Micro Dad, then pulled back his hand and turned to stare at Phil. "I was trying to apologize."

"Oh, yeah. We're good. Don't worry about it," Phil said without even turning back to look at Micro Dad, his mind only focused on flying. "Did you see that?"

"See what? I was looking at you, remember? My back was to the window."

"I saw something turn into that alley back there. And it didn't look like a red cell."

"Are you sure? How could you know what you saw from all the way up here? It could have been anything," Micro Dad said suspiciously.

"I'm sure," said Phil. "Trust me. I fly around the lungs every day. I know every single red blood cell here and that wasn't one of them. I know what I saw."

Micro Dad stood motionless. He wasn't convinced Phil saw anything. He was sure it had to be his imagination, but he was out of ideas. He had no choice but to trust Phil. "Well, in that case, let's go check it out," he finally said and carefully sat in his chair.

Phil quickly turned the wheel hard to the left and flew toward the thin alleyway that sat in between two factories. Once they reached it, Phil slowly guided the plane down lower until they hovered just above the narrow space. The plane crept along silently to avoid being detected, but to their surprise, the alley was totally empty. There was no sign that a virus or anything had ever passed through.

Their eyes studied every object as the plane sailed along, but they found nothing, nothing ducking behind a dumpster or slipping into a side door. Phil's jaw tightened as they flew. He was sure he had seen something, but his confidence faded with every passing second.

"Maybe I only saw what I wanted to see," Phil thought to himself. He turned to Micro Dad, who was still gazing down at the path with intense focus. He opened his mouth to speak, but Micro Dad quickly stopped him.

"Don't worry. We probably just missed it. It has to be around here somewhere, right? Keep your eyes open."

With that, Phil turned back to the alley and continued to search. They were near the end of the line. The wall of another building stood in front of them with only enough space to either turn left or right. They approached the split when suddenly, Micro Dad shouted excitedly.

"Did you see that?" he shouted.

"See what? What'd you see?" Phil asked, almost jumping out of his seat.

"I saw something turn that corner. Up ahead to the left."

Phil increased his speed slightly. When they rounded the corner, they immediately saw it. A short, grey figure moved sluggishly below them, clutching the wall on its left. It walked with an obvious limp, its feet scraping the ground as it went along.

"Got him," said Micro Dad triumphantly. "I can see his horn from here," he said, pointing down at the ivory-colored object sticking out of the figure's face. "Let's go."

"Wait," Phil said as he reached out to grab Micro Dad's shoulder, stopping him from standing. "That's not The Rhino. It's just one of his copies."

"Are you sure?"

"I'm sure. Every time The Rhino transforms a white cell into one of his copies, something about the copy changes. It happens every time. It can be a small change or a big one. You see that limp?" Phil pointed at the virus. "That's a pretty big change. The Rhino doesn't have that, and he would never be seen out in the open like this. It has to be one of his dimwitted copies."

Micro Dad hesitated before speaking. "Yeah, I guess you're right. What should we do now?"

"I say we wait and see where this copy is going. He might lead us straight to The Rhino," said Phil, gripping the steering wheel tightly, "then we get rid of him."

Micro Dad grinned softly. He held out a tight fist in Phil's direction and said, "Let's do it, PJ."

In return, Phil lightly bumped his fist into Micro Dad's. "Let's do it."

Chapter 18

Time slowed to a crawl as Micro Dad and Phil hovered above the slow-moving Rhino-copy for what felt like hours. They watched it wander past factory after factory, going unseen by red blood cells, who were focused only on their jobs. It huddled close to the factory walls as it shuffled. Its left hand traced the brick, using it as a guide as it moved. It never looked up to notice the hovering plane following closely above it.

A loud yawn burst out of Micro Dad, showing how tired he was of the stakeout. "How much longer should we sit here and watch him walk? I don't think he's really going anywhere. It's like he's out on an afternoon stroll with the wall."

"We have to wait for him to lead us to The Rhino," said Phil, sending an even stronger yawn back like a game of ping-pong.

"But it's sooo boring."

Phil scoffed, "I don't know what you mean. I love this stuff. Usually, stakeouts are full of excitement. It's the adventure and the thrill of stopping bad germs, but this one's a little different. There's no thrill here, but let's just wait a little while longer and see if he leads us somewhere."

"Fine," Micro Dad agreed, "we can wait." Then he sat back in his chair quietly but quickly sprang up like a jack-in-the-box. "But what if he knows we're following him, and he's leading us away on purpose?"

"You really think he's doing that?" Phil asked with a laugh. "Him? He barely knows where he is, and you think he's capable of doing that?"

"It makes sense. The weakest copy tricks us into following it away from The Rhino's hideout just so the real Rhino can destroy more stuff. Because we think it's too stupid to know we're following it. It's probably never going to stop anywhere. Think about it," Micro Dad said with a grin while pointing to the side of his head.

Phil turned and looked down at the copy again. Unexpectedly, the copy slowed down and came to a stop outside a large rust-colored factory. It guided its hand across the wall until it reached the square door then tapped softly in a sort of pattern, sounding like a woodpecker tapping into a tree. The door swung open seconds later with only darkness inside. The copy slowly limped in then the door slammed shut.

"So much for your theory," Phil said with a smirk.

"Well, I'm right most of the time," Micro Dad said with a laugh. "Now, let's go down there and see who's inside, shall we?"

"Way ahead of you." Phil set the plane to autopilot and jumped out of his seat and sprinted down the steps toward the exit. Micro Dad quickly followed and met Phil at the door. He was already tying two ropes to a large hook connected to the side of the plane.

He opened the hanger door and tossed the ropes out onto the ground. "After you," he said, handing Micro Dad one of the long cords. "Don't be scared. Just hold on tight. You'll be fine."

"Thanks for the advice," said Micro Dad, taking the rope in his hand. Then without any hesitation, he jumped and slid down effortlessly with one hand. He made it down in seconds then looked up and flashed Phil a cocky smile as he waved.

"What a show-off," said Phil. He took a small step back then dove forward out of the plane. He was in a free fall right next to the rope, then, just before hitting the ground, he grabbed the rope and flipped, making a full circle twice before letting go again, twisting into the air then landing perfectly on both feet with his arms raised like a gymnast.

"What a show-off," Micro Dad whispered.

They crept up to the factory. There was only one window, which hung high in the middle of the single door the copy had entered through. Phil followed closely behind Micro Dad, and once they reached it, they stood on the tips of their toes to get a look inside. All they saw was darkness, but suddenly, a dim light flickered, then brightened, showing a room filled with The Rhino's copies.

Chapter 19

The Rhino stood in the shadows at the top of a lengthy set of stairs. He remained quiet and motionless as the crowd talked to one another below him. The conversations were soft and low, but the hundreds of copies in the room made the space sound like a swarm of rustling flies. The Rhino soaked it all in. He loved seeing the massive army he had created.

He and his copies had taken over the factory days before. The building sat between two high-level factories and was large enough to house all of the virus's copies. The Rhino was so sneaky when he took over the building that none of Alex's cells even noticed that it had fallen under his control. It was the perfect hideout.

He especially enjoyed seeing his army together inside the lungs, right under the cells' noses. He smiled down at them all as if he were a proud dad. After a few moments, The Rhino stepped forward to the edge of the final step. The smile disappeared from his face, and only a grim, humorless expression remained. It was the look of a leader preparing to rally their troops, the look given before war.

The copies continued with their chatter, seemingly unaware of The Rhino's presence, then suddenly, The Rhino raised his hand into the air. He didn't make a sound. A hand was enough to get every copy's attention. In a split second, the copies stopped speaking, some while in the middle of a sentence.

They all rotated to face their leader, instantly forming lines across the factory floor. They stood perfectly still with their backs completely straight, all except the one limping copy who had to lean on a nearby wall to keep itself balanced. Each soldier stared at The Rhino, waiting for his orders.

The Rhino lowered his hand gradually then cleared his throat to speak. His voice came out surprisingly warm and gentle. "Soldiers, today is a great day. Today we make history." He took one step down. Each of the copies' piercing black eyes moved as he did. "I invaded this city known as Alex only days ago and look how far I've come. I've transformed countless of white blood cells into you, you, my copies, my soldiers. We have an army. One strong enough to completely destroy this entire city."

The copies remained motionless, but their small eyes grew bigger and filled with excitement the more The Rhino spoke. "With your help," he continued, his voice gaining charisma with every word as he pointed across the wide factory at the viruses, "we've destroyed the sinuses. We've caused destruction in the throat. And I singlehandedly wrecked headquarters in the lymph nodes." Immediately the room filled with excitement. Bursts of cheers and applause erupted from the audience.

After a moment, The Rhino raised his hand. Silence immediately followed. "I'm glad you're all in such good spirits, but our work here isn't done yet. We've taken over this factory for one reason and one reason only. Today we destroy the lungs, and with it, this entire city!"

He slammed one fist into the other, making a loud bang like a clap of thunder that echoed across the silent room. Beads of sweat dripped down his round cheeks and crashed on the steps while he made his way closer to his audience.

"Everyone looks down on us. On me. They call me the 'common cold'. They actually use that word. 'Common'. Like

I'm nothing but an annoying pest that's too small and insignificant to be taken seriously. Just something to get rid of in a day with a little medicine. Well, after today, they'll treat me with some respect. After today, The Rhinovirus will be more than just 'common'. I'll be talked about with the greats, like Smallpox or Ebola!"

An eruption of applause began again. The Rhino stretched his arms wide to catch the admiration. He only ever received it from his copies but always craved it from everyone else. He allowed the praise to continue for almost a minute then finally stopped it with another raise of his hand.

"Soldiers, you had your assignments. Each of you broke into a factory here in the lungs. Have you all planted the bombs I've given you?"

The copies all answered as one, "Yes, sir!"

"Good," The Rhino said, a grin taking over his face, exposing his stained teeth. "Every factory will be destroyed with one press of a button, using this." He removed a small object from the pocket of his dirty cargo pants and held it out to show the mesmerized soldiers. It was square and black and had a single red button in the middle.

"This is the device that will completely bring down the city of Alex," he continued. "Once I hit this button, every factory will be destroyed. There won't be any more oxygen available for the red cells to deliver to the rest of the city."

Soft *ohhs* and *ahhs* floated across the room as the copies stared at the detonator in The Rhino's hand. They leaned toward him, their eyes wide, waiting for him to press the glowing button.

Feeling the anticipation, The Rhino hurriedly placed the device back into his pocket. "Be patient, soldiers. I can't press it yet. We need to be a safe distance away first. Once we arrive back at the nose, I'll set off the bombs, then we'll make our escape and infect another human. I heard Alex has a little sister." Then he laughed deeply, his big belly bouncing as his laughter infected the copies around the room until they were all laughing wildly.

His hand went back up after a few seconds, then the crowd once again fell silent. "We leave in fifteen minutes. Soldiers, be prepared; from this point on, everyone will fear The Rhino. It starts today!"

Chapter 20

Micro Dad and Phil listened closely to the theatrical speech while peeking through the window from the alleyway, their eyes wide and mouths hanging open. The hair on Micro Dad's arms stood tall during the parts of the speech in which The Rhino stirred up the crowd. He knew it would be tough to stop The Rhino but had had no idea his army was so large or that his willingness to destroy Alex's lungs was so strong.

Phil listened and swelled with anger. The Rhino insulting all white blood cells and boasting about destroying the entire city of Alex infuriated him. He wanted to pull the door from its hinges and fire a shot right at the virus. He reached for it, but Micro Dad quickly caught his hand as it fell on the handle.

"What do you think you're doing?" Phil snapped at Micro Dad.

"No, you're the one who needs to explain. Don't be crazy," Micro Dad said, pulling his hand away from Phil's, "we can't take on that entire army by ourselves. The first thing we need to do is get that remote. He might blow up every factory in the lungs right now if he saw us coming. I know you're mad, but we need to be smart about this."

Phil turned to Micro Dad then lowered his eyes to look down at his feet. "Who does that ugly grey marble think he is? I can't wait to shut his mouth for good. But I guess you're right. I'd be making a mistake."

Micro Dad sighed then let out a soft laugh. "I'd be scared if

I were The Rhino and had to go up against you, PJ."

"So, what's your plan?" Phil asked intensely.

Micro Dad stole a glance through the window to see The Rhino's copies marching across the room and packing their things, then he ducked down once again and whispered, "I think I can shrink and slip into the factory to get the remote, but just in case I can't, we need to get every bomb out of the factories as soon as possible."

"How can we do that?" asked Phil. "There're only two of us."

"Call for backup? Don't you have a radio or something?"

"I do," Phil said quickly, then he reached into his pocket but only found old candy wrappers. "It's not here."

"Well, where was the last place you had it?"

"At headquarters. I pulled it out my pocket before I started talking to Chief T. I wanted a piece of candy, so I set it on the desk next to me then—" Phil's voice trailed off.

"Did you pick it up? Is it on the plane?"

"I left it on the desk. It's probably halfway across the lymph nodes by now after The Rhino's bomb launched it out of HQ."

"Oh," said Micro Dad, holding back his laughter.

"That's not funny," Phil said with a straight face. "What are we going to do now?"

Micro Dad stood silently, thinking. "You'll have to fly back and tell Chief T in person," he finally said.

"What? I'm not leaving you here by yourself. I can't. Remember, I have to follow Chief T's orders."

"I don't see any other way, PJ. It's either disobey orders or let the lungs get destroyed. Besides, you fly so fast that you'll be back here in no time. We need to get the bombs out of all the factories. ASAP."

Phil took a few seconds before speaking. "All right. I'll go. But be careful. Don't get caught."

"I won't," said Micro Dad calmly. "Hurry back so I can watch you take down The Rhino."

Phil nodded and smiled. Then he sprinted to the waiting plane and quickly climbed the rope that hung from it. Seconds later, Micro Dad watched as the aircraft slowly crawled then sped back toward the entrance of the lungs.

Once Phil's plane was out of sight, Micro Dad peered into the factory through the small window. Most copies were still moving around the room, preparing for their escape to the nose, but five large bowling ball-sized copies huddled closely together near the door and enthusiastically discussed their leader's brilliant speech. None had their eyes on the door, so Micro Dad grabbed the knob with his left hand while keeping the other just above the shrinking button on his wrist, waiting for the perfect moment to press it. He took a deep breath, and in one motion he pulled the door open and pressed it.

The copies all whipped their heads around in a flash to see waves of light pouring in from the alley. They ran to the door then looked left and right, hoping to catch a snooping red blood cell in the wrong place at the wrong time, but they found nothing. The alley was completely empty, so they went back inside and slammed the door.

"Must have been the wind," said one.

"What wind?" another asked.

"We're in the lungs, remember?"

"Oh yeah. Right."

They walked back to their circle and went on with their conversation, but one unknowingly carried a hidden passenger on the inside of its muddy sandal. When Micro Dad shrank, he waited at the edge of the rusted doorknob for one of the five copies to walk back inside the factory. When the moment came, he dove off the edge and sailed through the air before landing on the copy's jeans, sliding past the wrinkles and set-in stains that clung to them, landing hard on the copy's dry, cracked foot.

It was a grey desert, desperate for moisture. The ashen foot was like burnt charcoal. Flakes of dry skin peeled off and bounced across it like patches of tumbleweeds.

Micro Dad ran and leaped over dry cracks that spread across the foot like dried-up streams. He ran toward the rubber strap that sloped down its toes. Once he reached it, he climbed to the top before the copies could re-form their circle.

He slid down the thin strap and landed on the copy's huge, dirt-covered big toe. When he landed, Micro Dad immediately sprinted as fast as he could. He focused on the approaching cliff made up of a jagged toenail, being careful to choose each step wisely. He had to time his leap perfectly or risk falling onto the factory floor and into a sea of copies that could squash him like a bug.

Once he was near the top, he took out a grenade, dropped it at his feet and continued running. The grenade rolled backwards down the nail for a moment before exploding, sending a shockwave into the core of the copy's toe. Micro Dad's foot landed at the tip of the nail just as the copy kicked out its foot wildly, flinging Micro Dad into the air.

"What was that?" the copy shouted and reached for its foot. The others stared at it suspiciously.

Micro Dad soared into the factory air. He was so high he could see every inch of the large room. He stayed calm and searched for his next target. His eyes dashed from corner to corner as he hung in mid-air then plunged to the ground.

Suddenly, he heard The Rhino's strong, gruff voice. He quickly turned and glanced over his right shoulder and saw the short, heavyset virus standing back at the edge of the stairs on the second floor. The Rhino was shouting at one of his soldiers for moving too slowly. He hurried the copy along then barked orders at his three best copies, and personal guards, as they stood a few steps below him.

Micro Dad knew he had to find a way to get up the steps before The Rhino was gone. He continued to search as he sailed down further and further until he finally spotted an unusually large copy marching slowly up the steps. Each of its feet slammed hard against them, making them all tremble as it walked. Micro Dad knew instantly that it was the perfect target, one big enough to land on like a giant runway.

In a hurry, Micro Dad shifted his weight toward the steps and pressed his arms flat against his sides until he formed a straight line. He was still too high and too far to reach the copy, but the dive helped him travel as fast as an arrow piercing through the sky. Within just a few seconds, he closed the gap and approached the hefty copy.

It was nearly at the top of the stairs. Micro Dad looked at The Rhino. He was still giving his three guards orders but was inching toward an office door.

A tiny flash of white and blue zipped past as Micro Dad fell. He was close to crashing into the copy like a meteorite, but at the last moment, he opened his arms, catching the air. He floated down with less and less speed as he entered the copy's atmosphere then flapped his arms and legs as if he were in a swimming pool until he reached his target. He could have easily landed on the copy's huge stomach or plump head, but he decided to go for a better option.

He sailed toward the copy's large horn but dropped too fast and landed hard. His knees buckled on impact, and he lost his footing and fell backwards. Struggling to stand, his feet searched for solid ground. His boots slid on the smooth surface of the horn until he found his balance and stood up just in time.

The copy had reached the top of the stairs. It was just a few steps away from The Rhino. The three guards were the only thing that stood between them. They were still listening to The Rhino closely and didn't notice the large copy until the light behind them dimmed and an enormous round shadow formed in front of them. The Rhino's booming voice faded as the copy nervously interrupted.

"Excuse me, sir. I'm sorry to interrupt," the copy said in a low murmur, "but my things are all on this floor. Could I please get by?"

The Rhino looked at it with narrow, piercing eyes and said nothing for a few moments. He stared hard at the copy then cleared his throat and answered, "Get your things, soldier," as he nodded to his guards. "Let him pass."

The guards stepped to both sides of the thin stairway to clear a path. The copy marched up the steps as quickly as it could, but even by itself, it barely fit in the narrow space, so it had to hold its breath, suck in its gut and squeeze past the three guards. They all stood as tall and straight as possible. They nearly sat on the handrails to avoid being bowled over by the sizeable copy. Only traveling four steps, its body scraped against theirs the entire way, almost knocking them off.

Once it reached the top, the copy stood in front of The Rhino. It straightened its back perfectly and raised its right hand to the top of its head.

"Excuse me, sir," it said.

The Rhino returned the salute but didn't step to either side to let the copy pass easily. He casually said, "As you were, soldier," and stood firmly planted to the same spot.

The copy sighed and slowly walked away from the steps and past The Rhino, trying as hard as it could to hold in every bit of its stomach and avoid bumping into its stone-faced leader. It barely breathed as it moved. It shuffled from side to side like a crab, not even making eye contact with The Rhino.

But before the copy could pass, there was a moment when the two were so close that the copy's beach ball-shaped belly grazed the shorter Rhino across the chest. In that moment, Micro Dad saw his chance. The Rhino and his copy were almost touching, but to Micro Dad, it was a wide gap between the two heavy viruses and would be dangerous. It was his only chance.

Micro Dad took a few steps back to gather his speed. He was careful not to slide off. He took a breath and sprinted until he reached the horn's edge, then he planted his boots firmly into the ivory-colored ground beneath them and pushed off as hard as he could. His body immediately shot off like a spring.

If The Rhino had seen what was hurtling towards him, it would have only looked like a speck and not Micro Dad, the tiny superhero. He soared over the gap, rising higher and higher, moving through the air like he had been shot out of a cannon. His arms stretched in front of him, his hands ready to grab hold of whatever they touched as he began to fall.

As he dropped, Micro Dad gazed down and saw an object slowly taking shape in front of him. It became larger and clearer the farther he fell. Once he saw the sharp point resting at its tip, he knew right away that he was falling straight toward the top of The Rhino's horn. The razor-sharp tip was a light at the end of a dock, guiding Micro Dad straight to it. To him, it was like diving toward the highest and sharpest point at the top of Mount Everest, if Mount Everest were attached to a dangerously mean virus with the personality of a wolverine.

Micro Dad hesitated at first. He didn't know what to do. He was only seconds away from being speared. He thought hard then finally reached into his belt to retrieve the micro-plane, but just before gripping it, a rush of air came unexpectedly from up above. The large copy had finally let out the breath it had been holding while passing The Rhino. The heavy wind blew Micro Dad away from the jagged tip and across The Rhino's crystal blue left eye until he landed in the middle of his shoulder.

The landing was effortless, and Micro Dad wasted no time searching for an exit. He still had to make his way off the shoulder and to The Rhino's tattered jeans, where he could find the remote detonator in the pocket. He reached the shoulder's cliff quickly and gazed down to see The Rhino's white t-shirt flowing down in a stream of food stains, running right into his front pocket, where the slender black remote stuck out.

Micro Dad beamed.

"Piece of cake," he thought, then without hesitation, he stepped off the edge and slid down a deep wrinkle, zigging and zagging down the shirt like it was an amusement park slide. The path led straight to The Rhino's jeans. He slid easily into the open pocket and right on top of the detonator.

"This is too easy," he whispered then pulled a disk from his utility belt. He hurled it at the remote, and it immediately stuck to it like a magnet.

He rested his left hand on the remote and used the other to press a button on his wrist, but nothing happened. The remote didn't shrink. He pressed again and again, but the remote stayed large.

"Maybe this won't be as easy as I thought, after all," he groaned.

He had planned to shrink the remote and carry it away, but now, he had a serious problem. He had to find a way to sneak the detonator out of The Rhino's pocket without The Rhino or any of his copies noticing. It seemed impossible.

"How am I going to carry this thing out of here without anyone seeing?" he asked himself as he searched for an answer. Without warning, the pocket and everything in it began to shake as if it were in an earthquake.

The Rhino's jeans swayed from side to side as he turned to march to his office. He yelled over his shoulder as he moved. "I'm going to my office. I expect everything to be packed up and ready to go in ten minutes. Dismissed."

"Yes, sir," the three guards shouted back. Then they hustled down the stairs in a line, their feet hitting the copper steps at the same time.

Afraid of being trapped in an office with The Rhino, Micro Dad rushed to take the detonator. He jumped from the remote to the outer edge of the pocket. The ground under his feet continued to quake. He held on to the remote as tightly as he could, keeping his balance and avoiding falling over the edge.

The Rhino yanked the door open. It let out a long squeak just as Micro Dad gripped the detonator with both hands and pulled as hard as he could. The remote groaned but hardly moved at all. He pulled until his entire body stretched away from the device and hung in the air.

Suddenly, the detonator began to crawl out of the pocket slowly until only a small piece on the very end was left. Once it reached the pocket's ledge, the remote started to wobble. It fell back into The Rhino's pocket before shooting straight up then immediately sinking back toward Micro Dad, who was hanging from the other end. He gripped it even tighter and refused to let go.

It rocked back and forth twice, and on the last cycle, it leaned toward Micro Dad and slowly fell from the rim of the pocket. Without delay, Micro Dad lifted himself up onto the remote and laid down as flat as he could. He pressed his facemask and helmet against it as he waited for the ride to end. It was all he could do.

The remote picked up speed. It fell faster and faster toward the metal floor. It was in the open air and couldn't be stopped. It hit the floor with a hard thud. The sound of the crash was barely loud enough for any of the copies to hear, but to Micro Dad, it was like an explosion and almost threw him onto the ground.

After it crashed, the remote instantly skidded across the floor, sliding between the legs of two copies and nearly getting stepped on by a third. Every copy walked with their eyes focused straight ahead and never noticed the object skating underneath them. It passed another crowd before finally slowing down.

Micro Dad waited for it to stop completely before moving a muscle. Once it was safe and the remote stopped sliding, he opened his eyes and slowly lifted himself up. He looked around the room carefully, not knowing if one of the copies would come along and grab the detonator and him along with it. The remote had slid down the hallway and far from The Rhino's office door, but most of the copies had already marched down the steps, so the hall was completely empty.

Deciding the coast was clear, Micro Dad climbed down the back of the remote and landed on the metal floor. The shrinking disk was still attached to it, so he pressed the button on his wrist over and over again, but still, nothing happened. The remote stayed large and motionless. Micro Dad groaned and stared up at it. His foot tapped against the floor quickly as he thought of a plan.

He glanced over his shoulder and saw a nearby door. There was a narrow gap between it and the ground. The gap was small but possibly large enough to fit the remote through to get it to the other side. He didn't know what would be waiting for him there, but he knew it had to be dark since there was no light shining at him from underneath. He just hoped the space could hide him from the viruses while he fixed the buttons on his wrist.

He decided to take the chance. He took a few steps away from the detonator then sprinted toward it with his arms out in front of him. With one forceful push, he shoved it as hard as he could. It slid across the floor slowly. So, he did it again and again, the remote moving a bit more each time.

On his third attempt, he ran and drove his shoulder straight into the plastic. The remote glided across the floor like a hockey puck on ice. He didn't stop. His boots dug into the ground as he marched and pushed the detonator forward. Micro Dad moved inch by inch until he reached the door.

He stopped pushing once the front of the remote reached the narrow opening so he could catch his breath and examine the entrance. The gap wasn't very wide, but the remote was thin. Luckily, it passed the test and was just thin enough to slide right underneath.

Micro Dad got into position with his body shifted to one side and his shoulder up, ready to ram the detonator one last time and drive it into whatever was behind the door. His chest pounded from the workout. He took a deep breath then raced toward the remote. His shoulder landed with a loud crunch as he planted his feet into the ground and pushed.

The remote resisted at first, then it moved as if it had wheels.

It disappeared farther into the room. Micro Dad's feet shuffled one by one. His arm and shoulder were bulldozers, shoving the remote forward. He clenched his jaw until his mouth twisted into a snarl. Every bit of energy was focused on crossing the finish line.

The remote was halfway through the door when the left side of Micro Dad's neck tightened and cramped, so he turned to his right to ease the pain. Suddenly, a sound like metal scraping against itself screeched into his ears. It sounded close by and came from somewhere on his right side. He continued to push, keeping his mind away from the sound, but then he heard it again. He slowly opened his eyes and almost screamed when he saw what was there.

A dozen copies all sat at a table and watched the detonator slide across the floor by a seemingly invisible force. They had been eating lunch but stopped once they saw the remote moving by itself. Empty wrappers and crumbs were littered on the table, the group's faces, and their clothes. The stunned copies never made a sound. They were like ninjas but with plump round bodies that slumped in their chairs like slowly leaking water balloons.

One copy sitting in the middle of the cafeteria finally decided to see how the remote was traveling on its own. The sound of him pushing his chair back to stand up was the metal-on-metal squeal that got Micro Dad's attention. Once the virus was up, it moved with incredible speed, despite its size, and made it within steps of Micro Dad and the remote in less than a second.

Micro Dad tensed. He stared up at the copy then back at the door. He was only a few steps away from disappearing behind it and escaping, but the copy got closer and closer. Micro Dad could only watch it dart toward him. Its large frame towered over him in no time, and its hands quickly fell to grab the remote.

The copy's grubby hand reached lower and lower, its fingers wide like a claw, ready to snatch the remote. The race was on. Micro Dad pushed it as hard as he could. His boots slapped the metal floor as he sprinted.

It was neck and neck, but ultimately, Micro Dad won. The remote sailed past the door just as the copy's fingers swiped at it. Micro Dad followed closely behind and entered the dark tunnel through to the other side.

There was only darkness. A bit of light from the hall floated into the room from underneath the door, helping him to see just enough of what was in front of him. He looked up and found that fortunately for him, it was a closet. There were dozens of shelves full of sandals. The copies used it to store their extra pairs of shoes that were too disgusting to wear.

Suddenly, the doorknob started to rattle. The copy wasn't giving up. The door swung open, flooding the closet with light. The copy stood in the doorway and stared into the small space while seven others stood behind him. Micro Dad flinched when he saw the group. He stumbled forward, his left arm crashing into the back of the remote.

Immediately, light from the buttons on his wrist began to flicker. They flashed repeatedly until finally a solid bright light remained. Micro Dad gasped. He quickly placed his left hand on the remote and moved his right to press a button on his wrist. He knew he had to shrink the remote before the copy could get its hands on it.

Micro Dad reached out, but before he could press the button, a large hand soared down in the blink of an eye and scooped up the detonator. The remote floated up. Micro Dad rushed to grab the back of it with one hand as the other dangled at his side. It quickly went higher and higher until it left the closet. He held on tightly, his weight pulling him back down to the ground.

He had to find a way to get the remote back. His left hand clung to it. He reached up with his right hand, and with a shaky finger, prepared to press the button to shrink it. His finger almost made it, but the copy tilted the remote at the last second, causing the finger to jerk and push the wrong button. Micro Dad knew instantly he had made a mistake.

In a flash, his body grew larger until he was the same size as the copies that huddled around him. They were all instantly stunned. The detonator flew out the copy's hand that held it as its arms flung out wildly from the shock but remained in Micro Dad's, who was left hurtling to the ground before landing with a hard thud.

"Who is that?" a copy cried out.

"Where'd he come from?" yelled another.

The air left Micro Dad's lungs, and his face twisted in pain. There was a powerful ache in his back from the landing, so he didn't notice the copies slowly surrounding him until it was too late. He turned to the left to reach for the button to shrink out of sight, but he was stopped in his tracks.

Four large sandals appeared and pinned his arms to the floor. Then another pair landed on his chest, making it even harder for Micro Dad to breathe. The copy's heavy feet sat on his armored suit. He could barely move at all. There was a crowd of copies and no way to escape.

Suddenly, footsteps approached the chaotic scene. Micro Dad could feel them shaking the floor underneath him. They moved slowly but with power. They stopped right behind his head, blocking the light from above, which made it impossible for Micro Dad to see who it was.

The room quickly fell silent as everyone waited for the dark figure to speak.

"You must be Micro Dad," The Rhino said with a laugh.

Chapter 21

The three hulking guards guided Micro Dad into The Rhino's office. He was caught and forced to be their prisoner. The guards were far from gentle as they slapped handcuffs on his wrists then chained him to a large desk that sat in the center of the room. Once they finished, The Rhino calmly walked in and stood in front of the guards and Micro Dad.

"Outstanding work, soldiers," he said to the guards. "Leave him with me. You're dismissed."

"But sir, are you sure? He's dangerous," one of the three replied, sounding concerned.

The Rhino shot it a look filled with rage and answered, "And I'm not?"

"I didn't mean it like that, sir. You are. You're the most dangerous. It's just that, well, uh… He, he-he's, uh. We know who he is, sir. He's a legend. He—"

"Enough," The Rhino interrupted. "Leave this office… Now!"

The guards jumped into a line and quickly walked out of the office.

"And close the door!"

The last guard hurried back and shut it softly.

The Rhino turned to look at Micro Dad. A grin covered his face. He stepped toward him confidently, secretly proving to himself and his copies that he wasn't afraid. He even surprised himself by standing so close that he could touch him.

"So, you're Micro Dad, right?" he asked with a devious chuckle. "You know, THE Micro Dad. I've heard stories about you for a long time. You're a legend. I hear your name everywhere I go."

"I'm flattered. Really. It's always good to meet a fan," said Micro Dad, turning slowly from side to side to crack his aching back. Snaps and pops exploded from his bones. Once he finished, he looked The Rhino in the eyes. "Uh, that's better. So, are you that big of a fan to let me out of these cuffs?"

The Rhino laughed louder. "Oh, and he's funny, too! Incredible. I've heard a lot of tales about the great Micro Dad, but none of them ever mentioned you were a comedian." He turned his back to Micro Dad and slowly wandered around the room, speaking as he moved. "For years, us microbes have been hearing stories of Micro Dad. I always thought you were a myth. At least until I heard the story of you and your epic battle with pinkeye a few years ago."

Micro Dad thought again about his wife, Camille, and her crust-covered eyelids. Stopping that adenovirus was difficult, but he didn't think other viruses and bacteria gossiped about it. A small part of him wanted to smile from the recognition, but The Rhino continued.

"That's when I told myself if I ever met you that I'd be the one to destroy you."

Micro Dad's body tightened. "Why would you want to do that? Weren't you just saying how much I've inspired you?"

"Ha. Another joke. Good one," The Rhino mocked and continued pacing. "But it is true. You have unknowingly helped me become who I am today."

"And what's that?" asked Micro Dad. "Something that invades someone's body and transforms their cells into copies that are just like you?" he scoffed. "How could I have had anything to do with making you who you are? You're a virus. At best, you make people sick and annoy the heck out of them, and what's worse, you destroy people's lives."

"That's why you're here, right?" The Rhino asked, pointing a finger at Micro Dad. "You're the exterminator, right? Isn't that why you're here?"

"That's right. You're making Alex sick. I'm here to send you back to where you came from and clean up the mess you made so that Alex can feel better and do something that's important to him."

The Rhino's face suddenly grew serious. "Back to where I came from? And where would that be? I have no home!" he yelled, causing the office door to rattle. "I've always traveled from place to place looking for a home, but I was cast out every time. White blood cells got rid of me and didn't even try to get to know me. That's what happens with germs. We're constantly attacked for no reason at all."

He circled the room and stood halfway between Micro Dad and the door. "There's a war against viruses and bacteria," he continued. "How many of us do you kill every day? Do you even know? That's why every germ I know dreams about killing you. I told them all that I'd be the one to do it, but even they doubt me! They say I'm too small and that I'm just a cold. No one's scared of a cold, right?" he spat. "That's why I've made it my mission to destroy as many of you as I can, starting with Alex."

Anger boiled inside Micro Dad, but on the outside, he was unaffected. He looked down at his wrist and thought about how to get to it. His eyes moved around the room, thinking of a plan. As if he were reading his mind, The Rhino laughed and interrupted Micro Dad's scheming.

"There's no way you can escape, Micro Dad. Don't try. What makes this even sweeter is that I get to kill two birds with one stone. I'll be remembered forever by every germ on the planet once I get rid of you. I'll be remembered by all humans after I kill thousands of you before they even know it's me. It's genius."

The anger continued to simmer inside Micro Dad, but he couldn't help but laugh softly to himself. "That's a pretty big ego for such a tiny virus."

The Rhino tensed. His smile faded once again. "You won't be laughing in a few minutes," he said then whistled sharply. The piercing sound caused Micro Dad to cringe in his chains.

Without delay, the office door swung open, and The Rhino's three personal guards returned, but they weren't alone. This time, they wheeled in a rusted wagon with a large box sitting inside. Its tires squeaked as it rolled farther into the room. Once they reached Micro Dad, the guards gently lifted the box out the wagon and set it at his feet as if it were a gift. The trio immediately hustled out of the door, forgetting to close it.

The Rhino stared down at the box then up at Micro Dad. "Well, I've enjoyed meeting you, but it looks like this is the end of our conversation."

"Did you get me a gift for our first date? What's in the box, Rhino?" asked Micro Dad, afraid of the answer.

"I'm sure you already know," The Rhino replied coolly, "that's why you were trying to steal this." He pulled the detonator from his pocket and flashed it in front of Micro Dad. "There's a bomb sitting at your feet, Micro Dad, and in about five minutes, I'm going to press this button, and you'll be history. No more stories about you except this one after my bomb blows you to pieces and destroys Alex's lungs. Anything else to say? Any more jokes?"

Micro Dad's eyes locked in on The Rhino's. His expression hardened. And then with a perfectly straight face, he said, "That's the worst gift I've ever gotten," then he smiled brightly.

The Rhino tightened his fists. His face twisted in anger. His fuse was lit. He was getting closer to exploding in a fit of rage. "I'll show you. You won't be laughing in five minutes. You'll see. I'll make you all pay for laughing at me," he shouted. Then he marched out of the door and slammed it shut, leaving Micro Dad alone with a bomb at his feet that was only moments away from detonating.

Micro Dad tightened every muscle in his body and attempted to break the handcuffs off his wrists. The veins in his head nearly burst during the struggle. It didn't work. The chains didn't budge.

He searched the room for a way to remove the cuffs, but the room was empty except for him, the bomb, and the desk. It was more of a prison cell than an office. There was nothing he could use. He started to feel uneasy. He looked down at the buttons on his wrist and wished he could move things with his mind. That didn't work either.

He tried to force his arms together to stretch his right across to his left to touch any button on his wrist, but the handcuffs were too strong and held him back. His heart began to thump inside his chest. His mind raced even faster.

"Think, Micro Dad," he said out loud. "Think. You can figure this out. You've had to deal with more serious stuff than this. You can do it. Just think." His eyes shut. "Use your head. Just use your head. Use your—"

His eyes shot open, and he quickly stared down at his wrist. "Head!" he shouted.

He raised his arms as high as he could until he was doing a bad Frankenstein impression. He leaned his body forward as far as it could go. He lifted his head and dove face-first toward the buttons on his own wrist.

Instead, the facemask smashed into the bracelet of the handcuffs, missing every one of the shiny buttons next to it. He tried again but missed completely. His third attempt was closer. The side of his helmet lightly touched the corner of a button but not enough to activate it.

Frustrated, Micro Dad tried again. His arm stayed locked in place. He lifted his head and extended it as far out as it could go until he was as close as he could get to the dim light coming from the buttons. He eyed each one then used his helmet to peck at them, one-by-one.

After a few attempts, he found success. His helmet flattened one of the center buttons. He wanted to cheer wildly, but he quickly realized which one he had pressed.

"Oh, no. Not that one," he said, in complete disbelief. He shut his eyes and tensed his shoulders while he waited for the transformation, but nothing happened.

He stood up straight and looked down at his boots then up at the office ceiling. He was the same size. Micro Dad stared at the chains that clung to his wrists. It looked as if his only chance of escaping was gone.

His eyes remained focused on the handcuffs. Any glimpse of hope was fading quickly. Suddenly, he heard a small snap like a branch breaking in the woods. It grew louder until all Micro Dad could hear was crunching and breaking.

The handcuffs around his wrists became tighter. Within seconds, small cracks began to appear all over them. The cracks grew bigger and began breaking like glass.

Micro Dad's eyes studied the room. The door, the desk, everything became smaller. The room started to shrink around him. His arms and legs grew longer. His feet and hands grew larger.

The handcuffs continued to rattle and crack. The metal growled as it slowly broke apart. Unable to withstand Micro Dad's expanding body any longer, they shattered from his wrists and fell to the floor. He was finally free.

His arms flew into the air in triumph, but he was suddenly surprised when they brushed across the ceiling. His eyes shot up toward the rapidly approaching roof then back down to the floor that became smaller the more he grew.

Panicked, he fumbled for his wrist until his fingers found the correct button. He pressed it just as the top of his head touched the hard metal. He was close to bursting out of the factory like an overgrown tree. Incredibly, he shrank back to the size of a cell just in time but remained at the peak of the ceiling until he dropped and crashed onto the floor.

He stood up immediately and stared at the office door, certain The Rhino or one of his copies had heard the commotion and would walk in at any moment. He dusted off his armor and waited for one of the viruses to enter the room, but after a few seconds of waiting, he relaxed. No one came. Micro Dad couldn't hear a sound on the other side of the door. The Rhino's large army was either extremely quiet or they were already gone.

He took a step toward the door but was immediately stopped in his tracks. The front of his boot crashed into something that was as hard as concrete. His eyes dropped to the ground and saw the brown box that held the bomb. Micro Dad almost forgot to breathe as he froze, expecting the entire room to explode into flames.

His heart nearly stopped. He could only stare down at the box and hope the bomb would stay calm long enough for him to think of a plan. Seconds passed without the device exploding. Micro Dad hesitated then reached into his utility belt and removed another disk. The disk fell from his hand and landed on the top of the box lightly, gripping it as if it had suction cups attached.

He pressed a button on his wrist, and without delay, the box disappeared. He kneeled down and searched the floor for the package until he found it. The box was a tiny speck in an ocean of rust-colored metal. He picked it up gently with just his index finger and thumb and placed it in the center of his other hand.

It instantly stopped being an intimidating bomb and became as harmless as a birthday candle. He tucked it away in his utility belt for safekeeping then tiptoed over to the door. His helmet pressed against it, trying to detect even the slightest sound from the other side, but he still heard silence. There wasn't even a whisper.

Taking a chance, Micro Dad reached for the doorknob. He turned it slowly, afraid of making a sound. He could only hear his heart thumping in his chest. He opened the door slowly, letting in a small piece of light.

Without warning, a deafening sound, like an explosion, erupted from somewhere in the factory, echoing across the building with a BANG!

Chapter 22

When The Rhino left Micro Dad alone in the office, he marched downstairs in a huff. One copy after another saluted him, but he gave them no attention. He shoved past them all angrily, using one hand to push away his copies while the other hung at his side, balled into a fist. His lit fuse was getting shorter.

"He didn't take me seriously," he muttered under his breath. "How could he not take me seriously?"

He started to pace back and forth across the middle of the factory. His three guards followed closely behind him as he moved. They mimicked his every step but said nothing.

"He's like every germ I know. They won't take me seriously because they think I'm too small. Is that it? I'll show them. I'll show them all!" he hissed then suddenly turned, slamming into a passing copy, knocking it to the floor.

"I'm sorry, sir," the copy said instantly. It immediately got to its feet and stood at attention to salute The Rhino. "I should have been watching where I was walking."

That was all it took for The Rhino to explode. But it was less like an explosion and more like an angry preschooler having a screaming match with themselves. Shouts filled the room. His feet kicked the floor. The sounds were so loud that several copies thought they saw the desk lift off the ground upstairs in the office.

The outburst lasted for a little over a minute. When he finished, he cleared his throat and calmly asked the copy how long before their departure to which the copy quickly responded,

"Five minutes, sir."

The Rhino nodded in agreement. "Very good, soldier. Carry on," he said before adding, "I don't want to hear a peep from any of you until after we board the ships."

Each of his copies were used to the endless tantrums. They knew it was only a matter of time before he forced them all into complete silence, so they stayed quiet throughout the entire outburst. Any sound from the copies would have just made it worse for themselves.

The Rhino calmly walked away as if nothing had happened. With his guards in tow, he began to walk up the steps to get one last look at Micro Dad. The Rhino's feet had barely touched the third step when, without warning, there was a loud bang in the distance behind him. The noise echoed across the factory. It was like a clap of lightning and made The Rhino flinch.

He spun around so fast that he almost slipped and fell down the steps. Luckily, his guards caught him and helped him stand upright. Once he found his balance, they, as well as every other copy inside the building, searched for the source of the blast. Hundreds of eyes quickly focused on the factory's back door. It was blown completely off its hinges, leaving a large hole.

Light from the outside streamed through the building. The rays struck the copies. Some shielded their eyes in panic. They all stood and waited, unsure of what was coming next.

Suddenly, metal canisters flew into the building from thin air. The cans bounced off the ground, spraying a pale smoke as they tumbled. The gas consumed the bright light, and within seconds, more canisters covered the factory floor, filling the room up with a blanket of grey smoke.

Many copies began to cough and wheeze. They ran across the factory, fighting to breathe. But several, including The Rhino and his guards, didn't move. They stayed rooted firmly to the ground. The Rhino even smiled despite the smoke masking it.

He could barely see in front of him, so he listened carefully. He heard sandals flopping against the metal floor and endless shouting. He heard his copies running in all directions and yelling orders at one another, which no one seemed to follow. The Rhino casually cleared his sandpaper-like throat.

"Take your positions," he bellowed.

The noise ended quickly, and the room fell silent, giving The Rhino a chance to hear what was coming. His ears perked up. The floor began to rumble as if a herd of buffalo were approaching. The sound of boots colliding with the metal floor grew louder. The smoke began to fade gradually, exposing the hole in the wall. From both sides of the doorway, white blood cells stormed into the building, led by Phil, whose spotless white vest and helmet shined in the light that leaked into the room.

He and his team moved steadily with their knees slightly bent and their bodies tilted forward. Their weapons sat on their shoulders and pointed forward. They all carried the largest and best weapon ever made for white blood cells, the Germ-Crusher 3000. It was powerful and built to destroy any germ.

The Rhino's copies quickly formed a protective wall around the steps he remained rooted to. He sank just a little behind the wide handrail. Their weapons were old and worn, since they were found in the junkyard inside Alex's stomach. Even though they were old, the weapons were ready to fire at the first sight of a white blood cell.

One-by-one, the cells entered the building, moving past large pillars that stood erect throughout the factory. They huddled together and moved as a single unit like a school of fish, searching for The Rhino and his army. Once they reached the middle of the room, Phil held up a closed fist to give his team the signal to stop and hold their positions. A thick cloud of smoke began to slowly disappear in front of him, revealing dark round shadows on the other side.

A small gap was the only thing that separated the two armies. With every passing second, the rivals became clearer. Both sides stood their ground and waited for the chaos that was sure to come.

A rookie white cell stood beside Phil in the front of the group. It was his very first mission since finishing the academy. He was terrified but tried not to show it. His hands wrapped tightly around his weapon to stop them from trembling. But it didn't seem to work. Sweat poured out of them, making it even harder to grip its shiny silver.

His hands shook even more while staring out past the thinning smog and at the emerging figures. Their grey skin, tattered clothes, and ivory-colored horns seemed menacing. The rookie's finger inched closer to the weapon's trigger. He looked out at the army of dangerous viruses. Their horns gleamed like sharp knives, adding to the rookie's fear. He suddenly shuddered and his finger squeezed the trigger.

A beam of light the shape of a marble fired out of his Germ-Crusher 3000 as the shot rang out across the factory. It bounced off the metal walls and floors repeatedly. Viruses and cells ducked immediately. All but one. A copy in the first row groaned and snorted in pain.

Phil glared at the rookie and shouted, "I didn't say to fire!"

The copy breathed heavily as it stood frozen in place. Its nose moved wildly to take in air, but the freeze took over, stopping even that. The copy became a statue. Seconds later, every inch of it crumbled into countless pieces, becoming a mound of grey dust. It sat in a pile on the floor then was carried away by a soft breeze. The building was quiet enough to hear the wind drift by.

The viruses exploded into roaring shouts. The Rhino's voice rose above them all, "Attack!" as he lifted his weapon and fired.

Two beams of light exploded out of it. One soared above the white blood cell army, completely missing its mark, then vanished into the air. The other found a target. Phil turned to see a T cell get struck in the leg. The cell barely moved at all.

"Are you okay?" Phil shouted.

"I'm fine," the cell said quickly, not showing any signs of distress, but his face instantly twisted when he looked down and saw his leg. It was already growing. It doubled in size in less than a second, filling with fluid. The swelling quickly traveled up his leg to the rest of his body. Every inch of him grew bigger until he looked like a heavy drop of water. Phil could only stare as the cell suddenly burst, spraying the floor with plasma.

The factory erupted into chaos. A shower of small beams of light ripped through the air and battered the cells. One-by-one, white cells swelled then popped. Ten white cells quickly became puddles. The rest ran to search for cover.

Phil dove to the ground, falling hard on his stomach then crawled to find safety. He kept his head low to the ground and his eyes straight ahead as light zipped past him from all directions. He turned to see the rookie and many others firing back. They were hidden behind large metal beams throughout the factory.

Phil inched his way over to the pole where the rookie had his arms and half of his face exposed, firing at the viruses. Phil picked himself up and leaned against the metal beam once he reached it. The cold metal pressed against the back of his neck.

Seeing Phil, the rookie stopped shooting and fell beside him behind the beam.

"Sorry I fired too early, sir," he said while breathing heavily. "What do we do now?"

"Don't worry about it, Rookie. We can't stay here," Phil said calmly. "We need to move."

He stole a glance over his shoulder past the metal pole to see dozens of copies standing on the second-floor balcony, firing their weapons. Others hid underneath the staircase or took cover behind poles, spraying countless beads of light in the direction of the white cells. The Rhino and his guards never stopped firing as they slowly moved away from the steps. The cells were in trouble, and Phil knew it.

"We're pinned down, Rookie," said Phil. He looked to his left and right. Cells continued to get hit and explode into pools of liquid.

"They have the higher ground," he continued, "so we need to take out the copies on the second floor, but I need you to cover me while I run to that post over there to get a better shot." He pointed to a large pillar that stood between the staircase and their current position.

The rookie's face instantly turned pale. "You want me to cover you? But it's my first day. I have no idea what I'm doing. I barely made it through the academy. I don't think I can, sir. I'll call someone else o—"

Phil interrupted. "Listen to me, Rook. We have one job, and that's to protect Alex. If we lose, then Alex's lungs will get destroyed by this virus, and we can't let that happen. Understand?"

The rookie slowly nodded.

"It's all right to be scared. We're all scared, but this is our job. You can do this."

The rookie slowly nodded again.

"Now, when I count to three, you're going to cover me. Okay?"

The rookie took a deep breath before answering. "Okay."

Phil slung the Germ-Crusher 3000 across his back then turned and peered over his shoulder, waiting for the perfect moment. "Ready?"

"Yes, sir," said the rookie as he raised his weapon.

"One," Phil whispered.

The rookie slowly turned and peeked around the edge of the pole, aiming his weapon.

"Two."

"Three!" Phil shouted then quickly leapt from behind the metal and sprinted toward the next pillar.

Copies immediately spotted Phil running and took aim. Tiny beams of light filled the air around him as he ran. He was easy prey. They smiled brightly as they fired their weapons, but the rookie guarded him well. He fired one shot after another, turning the copies into frozen statues that quickly crumbled into piles of dust.

Phil made it to the pillar within seconds. He fell to his knees and slid the rest of the way just as a blast of light sailed over his head. He quickly stood up and leaned against the metal pole to catch his breath. His chest pounded. He wiped the sweat from his face as he removed the Germ-Crusher from his back.

The copies didn't stop firing at him, but their shots never found their target. Each burst of light bounced off the metal. Phil was well hidden, so he waited for his opening. Once the copies stopped, for only a second, he turned and fired his weapon up at the copies on the second floor.

He fired five times, hitting five copies. Each one fell to the ground then broke into pieces. After the fifth shot, Phil quickly hid behind the pillar to avoid the copies' next round of shots. After, he leaned out and fired several more times before taking cover once again. He did it again and again until there weren't any copies left standing on the balcony.

Without the copies firing from above, more white blood cells moved forward inch by inch. Led by the rookie, they marched deeper into the factory, ducking low to the ground while showering beams of light at the viruses. The team of white cells reached Phil, who stayed planted behind the large pillar, unable to move any further. They couldn't get to The Rhino and the rest of his army.

A dozen of the Rhino's copies kneeled behind the railing on the far side of the staircase and fired repeatedly at the crowd of white cells. The Rhino, his guards, and his other copies stood scattered throughout their side of the factory. Most hid behind pillars. Only the light streaming out of their weapons could be seen.

The two groups were at a standstill, but neither side gave up. Shots continued to ring out endlessly. Beams of light traveled in all directions, hitting nothing but the poles that stood in front of their targets. After a few seconds, the shots finally stopped on both sides, and silence filled the room.

"We're running out of time," Phil whispered to the rookie. "If The Rhino still has the remote, he could set off the bombs at any moment. We have to find a way to end this. Right now."

"But how?" asked the rookie. "We can't go any further without being exposed."

Phil fell silent and gathered his thoughts before speaking. "They have too much firepower, and they'll stay hidden. We'll never be able to draw them out. Unless…" his voice trailed off.

"Unless what, sir?" the rookie asked eagerly.

"Unless we give them something to shoot at. Bait," said Phil. "I'll run underneath the staircase and attack them from the right. They won't be able to resist shooting at me. While I have their attention, half of you go to the left side, and we'll surround them."

"But sir, that's crazy. You could get hit before you even make it to the stairs," the rookie said nervously.

"That's a risk I'm willing to take. I'll need you and the rest of the team to cover me while I run, understood?"

"But sir, let me go. I can—" The rookie attempted to interject but was quickly silenced.

"This is an order, Rookie. Spread the word."

Reluctantly, the rookie turned and got the attention of the remaining white cells who were hidden in groups behind nearby pillars. With just a few hand signals, he informed them of Phil's plan. The others didn't raise any objections. They all gripped their weapons and prepared to fire.

"Everyone's ready," the rookie said to Phil and aimed his weapon.

"Let's not waste any more time then," Phil replied tensely. "One."

"Two."

Without warning, shouts of pain echoed throughout the factory, one after another. Phil instantly stopped counting and turned to see if anyone on his team had been hit, but no one had. They all stared at each other with looks of confusion, completely unaware of what was happening. Again, shouts filled the room, but this time Phil could hear them coming from beyond the staircase where The Rhino and his copies hid.

Suddenly, booming shots rang out once again. Phil expected flashes of light to fly at him, but nothing came. He carefully peered out from behind the pillar and saw countless beams of light, but instead of sailing toward him and his team, the beams scattered in all directions toward the other side of the factory as if the viruses were shooting at dozens of new targets.

The viruses were under attack, but Phil didn't know by whom or what. Whatever it was, it drew the viruses' attention away from him and his team. The Rhino and his copies hadn't fired a single shot at the white cells for some time. So, Phil decided to move forward.

He slowly walked into the open. The other white blood cells hesitated but followed his lead. They slowly crept closer to the staircase, but before they reached it, Phil turned to the rookie and the others and motioned for them to surround the set of steps from both sides. Once they were in position, he turned his attention back to the middle of the staircase and moved closer.

He saw nothing as he approached it. No grey skin or horns. He raised his head slightly and leaned forward over the railing to get a better look at the other side of the staircase. As his eyes searched for a sign of the viruses, a beam of light appeared without warning and raced toward him. Phil could only watch as it zipped through the air and flew straight at his head.

Chapter 23

Before the burst of light could tear into him, turning Phil into a pool of plasma, a sudden flash of blue and white emerged from thin air. Phil immediately felt a jolt knock him to the ground just as the ball of light sailed over his head and disappeared into the factory air. His eyes shut as he hit the floor hard, feeling pain rush through him.

Soon after, he heard shots firing from all around him. Then he heard what sounded like white cells shouting until the voices were out of earshot. All except the rookie, who ran back to the other side to check on Phil. The first thing he saw when his eyes opened was the rookie smiling brightly at him.

"Are you okay, sir?" he asked.

"Yeah, I'm fine, Rook," Phil said with a slight groan. "What the heck happened?"

"He saved your life, sir."

"What?" Phil said in disbelief. "Who did?"

"You really should be more careful, PJ," Micro Dad said, moving to stand next to the rookie. "I won't always be around to save you." He flashed a warm smile then reached for Phil's hand to help him up.

Phil grinned as he accepted the help then got to his feet. "About time you showed up. Where've you been?"

"Well, when I heard you guys storm the factory, I knew you'd have the front covered. I figured the best thing we could do was to surround them. It took a while to sneak behind all those

Rhino copies, but they were terrified when I just popped up out of nowhere with my micro-gun." He held out the sleek weapon. "I froze dozens of them already. There aren't too many left."

"Did you get The Rhino?" Phil asked excitedly.

"No. I haven't seen him since he locked me in his office with a bomb."

"He saw you? Did you get the remote?"

Micro Dad shook his head. "I had it, but The Rhino took it before he chained me up. We have to get it back before he detonates the bombs. Have they all been removed from the factories?"

"Chief T has the entire force working on it," said Phil. "I'll call him to see how it's going." He reached into the pocket of his vest to remove a small radio then clicked it on before holding it to his mouth to speak. "Chief T, come in. Are you there?"

Within seconds, Chief T's rough voice spilled out. "I'm here, Captain. What's your status?"

"We have the viruses on the run, sir. It's only a matter of time before we defeat them all."

"Do you have The Rhino in custody?" Chief T asked intensely.

"Not yet, sir."

"Well, be on the lookout, Captain. This isn't over until either we have The Rhino in custody or we turn him into a pile of dust."

"Copy that, sir. What's the status of the bombs? Have they all been removed from the factories?"

There was silence for a moment before Chief T spoke again. "We've removed almost all of the bombs from the factories. We only have a few left. What's your plan to get rid of them, Captain?"

Phil hesitated then glanced at Micro Dad with a puzzled

look.

"Well, sir, I haven't really thought that far ahead yet."

Again, there was silence. When Chief T finally spoke, he did so tensely, as if he were speaking through clenched teeth. "So, you don't have a plan, Captain?"

Phil raised the radio to his lips, but no words came out. After a moment, Micro Dad signaled for him to hand over the walkie-talkie. Phil lightly tossed it over like a hot potato. Micro Dad caught it and cleared his throat.

"Chief T, this is Micro Dad," he said warmly. "Listen, I have a plan to get rid of the bombs. I need you to tell your team to stack all the bombs into a pile here outside the factory."

Chief T shouted without hesitation, "Micro Dad, are you crazy? The explosion with that many bombs would destroy every inch of the lungs. That's the opposite of what we want to do."

Micro Dad stood his ground. "Chief, you have to trust me. I have a plan. Pile every single bomb together. Let us know when it's done."

Chief T let out a heavy sigh. "We'll have every bomb stacked in front of your location in two minutes. Don't make me regret this, Micro Dad."

"I got you, Chief. Over and out."

Micro Dad tossed the radio back to Phil. "Ready?"

"I sure hope you know what you're doing," Phil answered.

"So do I," Micro Dad said with a laugh. "Now, let's go find The Rhino."

Chapter 24

Micro Dad, Phil, and the rookie rushed past the staircase and moved through the building until they found the team of white blood cells. They had the last of the invading viruses trapped in a small corner of the factory. Less than ten of the germs remained, but they fought like they were still a huge army. Bursts of light exploded from their weapons as they fired at Micro Dad and the cells.

The trio quickly ducked as the shots raced toward them. They took cover behind pillars with the remaining cell team. They all huddled together as if they were waiting out a storm, but the viruses were relentless. They never stopped firing. Any cell that was in the open and tried to fight back immediately collapsed into a puddle.

The viruses were backed into a corner, but there was nothing the cells could do to stop their attack. Their faces were grim and full of worry. They knew The Rhino could detonate the bombs at any moment while they stayed trapped. It seemed hopeless until one cell turned to see Micro Dad standing beside them.

"It's you!" the cell shouted when he saw the blue-and-white armor. "Guys, Micro Dad's here."

One-by-one, the cells lifted their heads to see the legend they had all grown up hearing stories about. Their faces instantly brightened, and their eyes soon focused on Micro Dad.

Feeling the weight of the moment, Micro Dad cleared his throat, placed his hands on his hips, and prepared to give a gripping speech. "Great job, everyone. There's nowhere for the viruses to go. I'll take it from here."

Phil snickered. "Was that it? Was that the whole thing?" he whispered to Micro Dad.

"Yeah, was that not enough?" Micro Dad whispered back.

"I thought there'd be more, since you put your hands on your hips like that."

"Every superhero has a cool pose, PJ. I can say more if you want."

"No. It's fine."

"Whatever. I'll work on it, all right? Anyway. I'll take it from here," Micro Dad said, gazing out at the group of cells.

"How do you plan on getting over there?" asked the rookie.

Micro Dad thought for a moment then smiled. "I'll need a push."

He reached into his utility belt and removed a red disk. It instantly turned the size of his palm.

Phil grinned. "Is this one of the shrinking disks, like back at headquarters?" he asked excitedly.

"No, this is just a frisbee," Micro Dad said with a laugh.

The cells muttered to each other in disbelief. "What are you going to do with that?" one asked.

Micro Dad turned to Phil and handed him the plastic toy. "Take this. I'm going to shrink to become small enough to ride it to the other side and surprise The Rhino. I just need you to give it a good toss to get me there."

Phil looked stunned. "You can't be serious."

Without warning, a ball of light struck another white cell, leaving a pool of plasma.

"Trust me, PJ. We're running out of time. We have to do this now," Micro Dad said anxiously. He leapt high into the air, spinning and flipping before vanishing.

The white cells gasped in amazement. Their eyes searched

the area for any sign of Micro Dad. Phil joined them but found nothing as he examined every inch of the floor around him. Suddenly, a glimmer of light flickered from the frisbee in his hand and captured his attention. He stared at it closely and saw the tiny speck of silver and blue holding onto the toy's rim.

"We're really doing this?" he asked with a sigh. "Well, you asked for it."

Phil snuck a quick glance behind the metal pillar. The viruses were still shooting endlessly. Beams of light scattered in every direction. He held the frisbee firmly between two fingers then threw it with a smooth flick of the wrist.

The toss was perfect. The frisbee glided through the air as if it had wings. It sailed above the stream of light then slowly dropped. When it landed, it skipped across the floor like a stone across a pond, then it crashed into the wall behind the unsuspecting viruses.

The sound startled the viruses immediately. They stopped their assault and stared at the disc. Their weapons sank down to the floor while they laughed hysterically and surrounded the frisbee.

"This is the best they can do?" The Rhino said with a huge grin. "They're throwing garbage at us?"

One of his guards snorted with laughter. "These cells really are pathetic. I'll send it back to them in pieces."

He reached down to pick up the disk, but as he leaned forward, a sudden burst of white light erupted, blinding the viruses. In an instant, Micro Dad appeared with the micro-gun gleaming in his hands.

"Don't move!" he shouted.

One tough copy ignored the command and raised its weapon. But before it could fire, Micro Dad aimed the micro-gun and squeezed the trigger. A ball of sticky slime exploded out of the weapon and hit the copy's chest, splattering on impact. In less than a second, the zinc in the mixture began to work. The mixture hardened like cement as it spread outward from the copy's chest until it covered every inch of the virus.

In a panic, another of the copies fired a shot but missed and hit the wall behind Micro Dad. He quickly spun and fired a shot of zinc at the copy, hitting it in the shoulder. The copy instantly became encased in hardened slime. In seconds, both copies crumbled to the floor.

Heavy snarls rumbled on Micro Dad's left and right. He turned to see one of The Rhino's guards and another copy grunting and stomping their feet wildly, ready to attack. With their piercing eyes locked in on Micro Dad, they lunged at him with their massive horns.

Thinking fast, Micro Dad pressed a button on his wrist and disappeared just as the two guards crashed into each other then fell to the floor. He reappeared in the blink of an eye then fired a shot at each of them before they could get to their feet.

Suddenly, The Rhino's last two personal guards, one on each side of him, rushed in and shoved Micro Dad intensely. He stumbled backward then slammed into the wall. One of the guards dove at him, its horn hurtling toward his belly. Micro Dad took a step to the right, narrowly avoiding the copy's horn. It lunged forward again but missed and rammed the metal wall, giving Micro Dad enough time to freeze the copy.

The Rhino's last copy leaped and knocked the micro-gun out of Micro Dad's hands with its horn. He watched the weapon drop to the ground then slide into the wall. Micro Dad dove toward it but was quickly tackled hard by the copy and landed on his back. The two struggled for a moment. The large virus was too strong and gained the upper hand in no time. It pinned Micro Dad to the floor, its body like an anchor on his chest, snorting loudly as it shook its head from side to side, attempting to slice through his helmet.

The virus continued to thrash, but Micro Dad grabbed it by the horn with both hands to avoid being speared. He held onto it for as long as he could then tucked his legs underneath the virus's bulging stomach, and in one motion, he pressed his legs up and gave the copy a powerful kick. It staggered backward then fell to the ground with a thud. Micro Dad quickly scrambled to reach the micro-gun. He grabbed it just as the copy got to its feet, then while lying on his back, he fired two shots of zinc. They both hit their target and froze the copy almost instantly.

Exhausted, Micro Dad breathed heavily then slowly sat up, using the micro-gun as support. But before he made it to his feet, the sound of The Rhino's raspy voice appeared behind him. It forced him to stop in his tracks.

"You destroyed all of my copies, Micro Dad," he said with a chuckle. "Well done. But you forgot one thing. I still have this."

Micro Dad slowly turned around and saw The Rhino. He had a large smile and held the small remote detonator in his hand. His finger hovered above the button that could trigger every bomb in the lungs with just one touch.

"Are you ready for the fireworks, Micro Dad?" he said, grinning from ear to ear.

Suddenly, the team of white blood cells rushed toward them with their weapons aimed at The Rhino.

"Don't move, Rhino. It's over. Drop the remote and put your hands up," Phil shouted.

The Rhino's smile quickly faded. "You don't give me orders, blood cell," he growled. "Maybe you didn't notice, but I'm holding the one thing that could destroy Alex's lungs in seconds."

Phil's eyes narrowed and his jaw tightened. "You're bluffing, Rhino. You wouldn't press that button while you're still in the lungs with us."

"You willing to find out?" The Rhino barked. His finger moved closer to the button.

"Wait!" Micro Dad shouted. "Maybe we can make a deal?"

The Rhino scoffed. "Pathetic. I don't make deals with people or cells."

"Well, there's a first time for everything," Micro Dad said as he slowly stepped toward The Rhino.

"Hold it!" The Rhino shouted. "Don't take another step."

Micro Dad froze and raised both his arms above his head. "Sorry. I'm just talking," he said calmly. "Didn't you say you wanted to be remembered by every germ forever? No one will ever remember you just for destroying one kid's lungs. You wanted to destroy thousands of people, right?"

The Rhino didn't answer, so Micro Dad continued. "If you press that button then your legacy ends here. Is that what you want?"

The Rhino's eyes moved around the room, searching for an answer. After a moment, he finally spoke. "Do I look stupid to you? You're saying you'd just let me go?"

"That's right," said Micro Dad without any hesitation. "If you give up the remote, we'll give you a plane and you can fly out through the nose right now. It's that easy."

"That's crazy," Phil roared. "Micro Dad, we can't do this."

"It's the only way, PJ," Micro Dad replied coolly then turned back to The Rhino. "Do we have a deal?"

"How do I know you won't shoot me or shoot down the plane once I'm on it?"

Micro Dad flashed a smile. "Trust me."

Chapter 25

Micro Dad and the remaining white blood cells followed closely behind The Rhino as he shuffled through the factory. He still held onto the remote with a finger resting near the trigger. The deal had been made with the one condition he be allowed to keep the remote detonator until he was safely on board a plane. Then, and only then, would he toss it to the blood cells and speed away.

The watchful cells kept their weapons trained on him as they marched. They were several steps away, but The Rhino could feel the weapons aimed at his back. Phil's eyes only left The Rhino occasionally to glare furiously at Micro Dad, who was strolling through the building next to the virus as if he wasn't holding a remote to activate hundreds of bombs. Within a few moments, the group reached the factory entrance. Waves of light shined through the large hole in the wall that the cells had created when they stormed in. They all stopped before anyone could take a step outside.

"After you, Rhino," Micro Dad said and extended an arm to guide The Rhino through the door.

The Rhino shook his head skeptically. "No. No way I'm walking out of that door first. I'll get shot if I stick one foot out there. I'm not falling for your tricks. You're going first, Micro Dad."

Micro Dad smiled lightly. "Where's the trust, Rhino? Fine. I'll go first," he said with a shrug then stepped out of the door.

The Rhino swallowed the lump in his throat then quickly

followed Micro Dad. He stepped close behind him, nearly pressing against his back. He kept his head down and mimicked Micro Dad's every move. He only occasionally turned back to see the white cells trailing.

The Rhino waited for them to make their move, his finger creeping closer to the remote's trigger, but after several minutes, nothing happened. The cells just stared back at him with cold, angry eyes as they walked. Suddenly, he heard a loud bang. It made his body stiffen, and he almost pressed the button, but he thought better of it. Instead, he glanced down to see a large box sitting at his feet.

The box quickly multiplied. The Rhino studied the ground below and saw dozens more. His eyes followed them as the boxes began to pile on top of each other. The Rhino couldn't believe what he saw. A giant pyramid made from the viruses' bombs was stacked high above him.

Panic instantly gripped The Rhino. "You found every bomb in the lungs and piled them all here? Are you crazy?"

Micro Dad shrugged. "You're the one holding the remote to detonate them all. Better be careful with your fat finger."

"Whatever," The Rhino snorted. "Where're we going, anyway? You said there'd be a plane. I don't see a plane. All I see are bombs."

His eyes stayed glued to the pyramid. He followed it, amazed at how large it was. The pile was so massive that its peak reached the top of the two nearby factories. The Rhino was horrified by the sight, but his fear doubled when dozens of white cells suddenly appeared on the rooftops of the two buildings. They all had their weapons aimed at him.

The Rhino panicked. "What's going on? I knew this was a trick." His finger moved closer to the remote's trigger.

"Wait!" Micro Dad shouted. "Just relax. I'll talk to them."

"You better make it quick," The Rhino hissed.

Micro Dad quickly stared up at the white cells and shouted, "Don't shoot. We've made a deal with The Rhino. He's free to go."

The Rhino's heart raced as shouts filled the air. The cells were furious. He could feel their hatred. The shouts didn't end until a deep, husky voice rose above the rest. The Rhino shuddered at the sound. Soon after, Chief T thundered past rows of white cells, marching to the edge of the factory's roof.

"There're no deals to be made with The Rhino. We don't negotiate with viruses. Rhino, drop the remote and put your hands in the air."

The Rhino's hand tensed, but Micro Dad responded right away.

"Stand down, Chief. The Rhino is the last virus left. The goal was to get rid of them to help Alex. That's what we're doing by letting The Rhino go." Micro Dad inched closer to the building. "There's a plane right over there. We don't have time for a standoff."

The Rhino's stomach twisted into knots. He watched Chief T take a step back then pound his heavy foot against the metal rooftop in anger. His finger quickly shot out and pointed down at Micro Dad. The words rushed out of his mouth like a tidal wave.

"Who do you think you are?" he yelled. "You may be some bigshot hero, but you're still a guest in the city of Alex. I don't take orders. I give them, so you better be quiet and follow my orders," he spat. "I allowed you to work with us, but you're technically an intruder, and you know what we do with them, right?"

Micro Dad was shocked by the Chief's show of force, but he

176

refused to back down. The two glared at each other, neither one wanting to give in. Chief T was the first to make a move. He turned to the team of white cells standing behind The Rhino and shouted, "Arrest The Rhino. Then arrest Micro Dad."

Chapter 26

Every cell gasped. Phil and the others continued to aim their weapons at The Rhino, but uneasiness showed in their faces. The Rhino's hand tightened around the remote, waiting for the cells to act. But unexpectedly, none of them moved in to arrest him or Micro Dad.

"I said arrest him," the chief shouted again. "Phil, that's a direct order, son. Arrest him."

Phil gripped his weapon. He glanced at Chief T then back at the Rhino. Even from high above, he could feel Chief T's piercing eyes burning into him while The Rhino just stared back emotionlessly. Not knowing what to do, Phil's eyes wandered until they landed on Micro Dad.

He was standing beside The Rhino. The two locked eyes, then Micro Dad gave him a quick wink. It happened so fast that Phil wasn't even sure he had seen it. He didn't know what it meant, so he stood motionless for what felt like hours before he finally spoke.

"Chief, I agree with Micro Dad," he said boldly. "I've wanted to catch him for days. I don't like it, but we need to help Alex get to that science fair no matter what it takes. We have to make a deal." Then he slowly lowered his weapon and aimed it away from The Rhino.

The chief's expression didn't change. He stared at Phil, disappointment in his eyes. He shook his head from side to side and glared at the rest of the white cells on the ground.

"Grab that germ and Micro Dad, right now," he ordered.

To his surprise, none of them moved. They looked at each other nervously for several seconds then lowered their weapons. Their eyes quickly fell to the ground, avoiding Chief T's stare. Immediately, a large grin fell on The Rhino's face.

"I guess I'm not getting arrested today after all, Chief," he joked. "I'll see ya later."

Phil watched with frustration as The Rhino slowly shuffled toward a waiting plane that sat nearby between the two factories. Its door was open, and a set of steps hung down to the ground. It was only a few steps away, but before The Rhino could take another step, Chief T called out.

"Rookie, this is your very first mission, right?" he said warmly. "Don't let this be how you start your career. Trust me. This moment will either make or break your career." The rookie quickly shot him a look. "You can either arrest him and be a hero in the city and make it to captain in no time, or you can refuse, and I'll kick you off the police force and make sure you spend the rest of your life cleaning the worst places in the body. Maybe I'll have you reassigned to the intestines or maybe the appendix. Which would you prefer?"

The rookie cringed. He looked at his team as if he were waiting for their advice, but they continued to stare at the ground, not knowing what to say. His gaze moved to Phil, who stared back at him but gave no response. He just looked at the rookie for several seconds then finally spoke.

"It's your call, Rook. The intestines are pretty bad, but this is the right thing to do."

Chief T shouted impatiently, "Time's up. What's it going to be, Rookie?"

Chapter 27

The rookie's head was spinning. A million thoughts ran through his mind. He was terrified of making the wrong decision. His legs trembled, and before he knew what he was doing, he began walking toward The Rhino. He raised his weapon and took a few steps forward.

The Rhino flinched. "What are you doing, you stupid blood cell?" he shouted. "Get back or I'll blow everything to pieces." He lifted the remote into the air, making a show of sliding his finger to the button.

Amazingly, the rookie continued to move forward. The two were just a few steps away from each other. He kept his weapon trained on The Rhino's right hand where he held the remote. He hesitated at first then shouted, "Drop the remote and put your hands up, Rhino."

The virus did neither. His hand remained stuck to the remote. The rookie looked around for help that never came then turned back to The Rhino. He opened his mouth to speak again, but The Rhino stopped him before he could start.

"Will you please stop this," he groaned, sounding irritated. "We both know you're not going to arrest me. You're out of your league, kid." With that, The Rhino tapped the remote.

The rookie's stomach dropped as if something heavy had suddenly landed inside it. His face grew stiff. He bit his lip to keep from yelling or crying or both. He wasn't sure. He felt like he could explode at any moment. He kept his eyes on The Rhino and spoke firmly.

"I'll count to three."

"Am I supposed to be scared?" The Rhino asked with a soft chuckle. "What happens when you get to three?"

The rookie remained expressionless. "I'll make you drop that remote."

The Rhino responded with only a smile.

The rookie's hands wrapped tighter around the Germ-Crusher 3000, then he began to count.

"One."

Everyone stood frozen.

"Two." The rookie remained calm and locked eyes with The Rhino, seemingly unnerved. Every white cell stared at the scene anxiously. The rookie paused for a brief moment then continued.

"Thr—" But before he could finish, Micro Dad leaped forward and kicked his leg out into the air in an arching motion straight toward The Rhino. It crashed hard into The Rhino's wrist, just above the remote, sending a sharp pain up it. The kick was like a bolt of lightning and instantly numbed The Rhino's arm. His fingers loosened, and the remote dropped from his hand onto the ground.

Everyone stared as it landed, realizing what had happened. The rookie was the first to act. He lunged toward the remote with one outstretched hand, ready grab it, but as he leaned forward, The Rhino was quickly on him. The virus moved as fast as a cat and closed the short distance between them in less than a second. His large, powerful hand gripped the back of the rookie's neck and yanked him upward with a hard tug. The rookie's fingers were only able to sweep across the remote, sending it sliding away from him.

The rookie shouted in pain. He held his weapon and attempted to twist to his right and fire a shot at the virus, but The Rhino saw it coming and used his other hand to knock the weapon to the ground. The Rhino squeezed his neck as a warning to the rookie to not move or suffer even greater consequences. In response, the rookie immediately obeyed.

Phil and the rest of the white cells in the alleyway sprang into action. They lifted their weapons and aimed at The Rhino. They tried to get a good shot, but every bit of the virus was hidden behind the rookie.

"Let him go, Rhino!" Phil roared.

"What? This cell broke the deal," The Rhino replied, then his fingers dug even deeper into the young blood cell.

"You think I'd let him arrest me?" The Rhino chuckled. "No way. I'm getting out of here on that plane, and if any of you try to stop me, I'll turn this cell into one of my copies. You wouldn't want that, would you? At least he'd look better."

The Rhino laughed again then glanced over his right shoulder. Micro Dad seemed to inch closer by the second. He stared intensely at The Rhino as if he were a lion ready to pounce. He prepared for another attack, but The Rhino noticed his movement and called out to him before he could strike.

"Hey, stop right there, Micro Dad. You wouldn't want another cell turning into a germ on your watch."

Micro Dad quickly froze.

The Rhino flashed a crooked smile. "I thought so," he said as he took a step backward. "Now, I'm going to back up until I get to my plane. No one try to stop me. I'm taking the rookie with me until it's safe."

Quickly, The Rhino stole a glance behind him. The plane was still there. A set of stairs hung from the open door and rested on the surface of the alley. But before he continued on, he whispered to the rookie.

"Before we go, I want you to pick up my detonator. And don't try to be a hero again."

Without fighting, the rookie did as he was told. With The Rhino following his every move, the cell lowered his body to the ground. The remote sat beside the pile of bombs, so he barely had to stretch out his arm to grab it. Once he had it, he picked himself up and stood in front of The Rhino.

"Good. Now, put it in my pocket," The Rhino said, gesturing to an opening in his cargo pants.

The rookie hesitated for a moment. He held the remote at his side and considered tossing it far away so that The Rhino couldn't use it to destroy the lungs once he was gone. Seconds ticked by while the rookie stood deep in thought. He just stared down at the detonator in his hand, unsure of what to do.

Sensing the rookie's plan, The Rhino tightened his grip. "I said don't try to be a hero."

Pain shot through the rookie's body. He immediately second-guessed his plan. He knew he was in no position to go against The Rhino. All he could do was comply. He shoved the remote into the pocket then hung his head, not able to look at the other white cells in front of him.

"Good," The Rhino said with a beaming smile. "Let's go." He tugged at the rookie as he took another step backwards.

No one blocked his path, but Micro Dad and Phil stood nearby, one on each side of him. He shot them both a look that said, "Stay back or else." The Rhino's grip remained strong around the rookie as he guided him backwards. They shuffled their feet inch by inch.

Moments later, they reached the steps of the plane. They were tall blocks, so it took The Rhino a moment to feel for the first step with his toes while hanging onto the rookie and keeping both eyes on Phil and Micro Dad. Eventually, he lifted one leg high enough to reach the step then slowly went backwards. He went from step to step with the rookie following his every move.

The rookie grew more nervous with every step. He wasn't sure if Micro Dad or the other white blood cells would try to stop The Rhino from getting on the plane, but he knew his life would be over if they didn't. He would either be turned into a copy or a puddle of plasma once the plane was safely in the air. He knew he had to get away, but he couldn't get free of The Rhino's grip, so all he could do was hope to be saved.

The two were halfway up the steps when The Rhino eyed Phil, who was staring back at him furiously, and for a split second, he thought he caught a glimpse of Phil's finger twitch and touch the trigger of his weapon. He tensed, but to his surprise, he had only imagined it.

No shot rang out. The Rhino looked down at Phil and smirked, growing more confident with every passing moment. He took another step. His wide feet glided backward, but before they could land, the heel of his foot grazed the edge and missed the step completely.

His weight, combined with the rookie's, carried them both down several steps. They were close to tumbling down the entire staircase, but The Rhino quickly saved himself by releasing the rookie. He shoved the cell as hard as he could, launching him down the steps while he fell backwards and used his hands to grip the railing and stop his fall.

The rookie curled into a ball and rolled down each step like a stone. He eventually reached the bottom then crashed hard onto the alley floor. His entire body quickly became limp on impact. Soon after, a wave of exhaustion washed over him. He tried to move but couldn't, so he just shut his eyes and welcomed the calming darkness.

Chapter 28

Fear immediately swept through The Rhino. He looked down and watched Micro Dad and Phil race toward the rookie. The cell's body lay motionless on the ground, his face flat against it. Phil called out to him but got no response. Micro Dad slowly turned the rookie on his back then shuddered at the sight of him.

The cell was nearly unrecognizable, buried underneath dozens of scratches. Everyone, including The Rhino, cringed at the sight. The wounds seemed to get worse every second. Micro Dad moved to check the rookie's pulse, but before he could, the rookie let out a small groan to show he was still alive. His eyes remained shut, but he managed to say a few words through clenched teeth.

"I'm fine," he croaked. "Did The Rhino get away?"

Micro Dad and Phil's eyes grew wide. They gave each other a quick look then glared over at The Rhino watching the scene play out from the middle of the staircase. Their enraged faces quickly pulled him back to reality. He suddenly realized that he had lost the only thing that had kept him safe from the white cells.

Phil and Micro Dad kneeled beside the rookie as they scowled at The Rhino. Micro Dad slowly stood up. He was barely off the ground when The Rhino darted up the steps in a flash. He only made it up a few when, suddenly, a shower of light rained down around him from all directions as the white cells fired at him from the rooftops.

The light struck the steps again and again but didn't touch

The Rhino. He managed to avoid every single shot. His short legs carried him as fast as they could go up the remaining stairs. He dove headfirst into the plane just as a beam of light flew over his head then disappeared.

He landed with a hard thud but quickly jumped back to his feet without hesitation. Bursts of light began entering the plane, searching for him. Desperately needing a way out, he spotted a red button that hung on the wall next to the door. Without giving it a second thought, he rammed his fist into it. Immediately, the staircase began to fold into itself, taking away each step one by one as the plane's door slowly began to close.

The Rhino didn't waste time. He turned and sprinted toward the cockpit and fell into the seat. Within seconds, the plane started up. It's engine roared, ready for takeoff.

Outside in the alleyway, Micro Dad stood over Phil, who was still kneeling beside the rookie.

"He's getting away, PJ!" he shouted.

Phil nodded then went to stand, but he hesitated. His eyes fell on the rookie. He was still motionless and badly injured.

"The Rook's hurt pretty bad, Micro Dad," he said gravely. "I'm going to stay and make sure he's okay."

A look of surprise washed over Micro Dad's face. "You sure?"

Phil nodded. "I'm sure. I can't leave knowing a cell on my team is hurt."

Micro Dad gave Phil a light smile. He reached into a pocket of his utility belt then removed a small tan bag. He tapped a button on his wrist and the bag grew in an instant. Micro Dad reached inside it and pulled out many tiny micro-disks.

"These will take care of those bombs," said Micro Dad.

He took a step forward and tossed the disks into the air. They rose high above the mountain of bombs then came pouring down over them like drops of rain. Each one immediately stuck to one of the explosives.

After the last disk fell, Micro Dad tapped his wrist. A sudden flash of white light appeared and washed across the alleyway. In an instant, the mountain of bombs was gone. A nearby cell walked over and glanced down at the large empty circle where the bombs had been. The cell stared at the ground for a moment until he found a small mound in the center.

The pile was the size of the cell's thumb nail. He carefully scooped each one into his hand, astonished at how small the bombs had become. He admired them for only a moment then sprinted to Micro Dad and placed the flakes into his hand, giving him a shy nod just before sprinting away.

Micro Dad took an empty bottle from his utility belt and gently shook the bombs into it. When he was finished, he placed the bottle back into his pocket.

"Alex's lungs are safe now," he said with a smile.

"Thanks," Phil said softly, "now get going. The door is almost closed, and you still have to catch The Rhino."

"See you back here," Micro Dad said, turning towards the plane.

Chapter 29

The plane slowly rolled through the alley. The steps were gone. They had disappeared below the frame of the door, and only a small gap remained before the door shut completely, leaving Micro Dad locked outside.

Micro Dad sprinted. His feet hit the ground hard as he chased after the aircraft. His face tightened. He was only a step away from reaching the door, but the gap continued to shrink and would be difficult even for Micro Dad to squeeze through.

The plane rolled faster and faster. The distance between it and Micro Dad increased by the moment. Quickly, he reached for one side of the doorframe and gripped it with one hand. Once his grip was tight, he stretched forward and grabbed the other side. Unable to match the plane's speed, his feet scraped the ground around him.

His eyes stayed focused on the closing door. The gap was barely visible, and the light from inside the plane was almost gone. While holding onto the frame as tightly as he could, he launched himself up toward it in a single motion. When he was close to crashing into it, he let go, then he reached over to his wrist and pressed a button.

Time slowed as Micro Dad shrank to almost nothing. The iron door instantly changed into a massive wall. The gap had grown as well. It became a narrowing pathway wide enough for Micro Dad to pass through.

He drifted through the air for a moment, unable to do

anything except enjoy the ride. The light's gleam from inside the plane called to him. It guided him past the opening and through to the other side.

Once he entered, he drifted for a second longer before losing every bit of momentum he had gained. He went from soaring like a bird to dropping like a brick. His body straightened as he fell. Just before crashing into the floor, he tapped a button on his wrist and grew again in a flash. He landed with a hard thud, sending an echo through the plane to announce his arrival.

The Rhino sat in the cockpit and fumbled with the controls, but his head snapped back at the sound of Micro Dad entering the plane. The two eyed each other until The Rhino turned back, visibly shaken. He grabbed the plane's steering wheel and pulled it back with a hard tug. In response, the plane quickly lifted off the ground and into the air.

Micro Dad had to grab ahold of two seats on his left and right to keep from falling backwards. The plane rose higher and higher. It moved like it was climbing a steep hill, eventually soaring straight into the air.

Eventually the climb was too much for Micro Dad. His hands slowly slid off the seats. He immediately sailed backwards as if he were getting pulled by a string. He reached for nearby seats, but his fingers could only graze them as he flew by.

The fall ended with Micro Dad crashing into the wall at the back of the plane. He landed with a thud and quickly felt the air leave his lungs and pain creep into his spine. His eyes shot open. Every bone in his body instantly ached, but he was sure he hadn't broken anything. The suit had done its job.

He stared down the aisle. He could see The Rhino sitting comfortably in his seat inside the cockpit. The virus was focused on increasing the plane's climb. Occasionally, he would glance back at Micro Dad and give him a sly smirk.

Fumes grew inside Micro Dad. He raised an arm then slowly brought it toward his waist. He groaned at first, but the growing anger inside him masked the pain he felt. He reached into his pocket and pulled out a tiny piece of silver. The small object had always reminded him of a game piece that would be used in *Monopoly*. He pressed another button on his wrist, and instantly, the silver piece turned into the micro-gun.

Without hesitation, he aimed the weapon then began firing it into the cockpit. The Rhino jerked his head back to stare at Micro Dad coldly. "Are you crazy? We'll both go down if you destroy the plane."

"I'm willing to take that risk. Are you?" Micro Dad asked with a grim smile, knowing he could use the micro-plane to escape if anything went wrong.

He fired three more times. The Rhino shrank low in his seat as the shots sailed past him. They nearly grazed the virus. Each one hit the large window in the front of the plane and the control panel underneath it then quickly formed a hard crust.

"All right. Enough!" The Rhino shouted then slowly pushed the steering wheel forward. The plane immediately began to fall until it leveled out completely.

Micro Dad slid down from the wall to the floor and fell to his knees. He stood up quickly then marched up the aisle toward the cockpit, his weapon in hand. The Rhino turned to see him hobbling forward then searched for the button marked "auto-pilot". He found it just as Micro Dad neared the center of the plane.

He pressed the button down hard. In an instant, the plane responded. The Rhino felt the wheel tighten underneath his hands. It resisted any movement he tried to make. When he lifted his hands, the plane continued to fly straight ahead.

The Rhino turned his head from left to right to crack his neck. Loud pops echoed throughout the cockpit. He stood up just as Micro Dad neared the last few rows in the front of the plane. He took his rusted weapon out of his waistband then strolled over to meet him.

Moments later, they stood face to face. Only two rows of seats divided them. Silence filled the space. They eyed one another, realizing they had been in a similar standoff not long before, but this time, there was no one else there to interfere.

"You don't give up, Micro Dad," The Rhino said, breaking the silence. "I expected as much from you, but you must have forgotten I still have this." He reached into the pocket of his jeans and pulled out the small detonator the rookie had placed into it.

Micro Dad laughed softly but tried not to show his joy. "No, I remember, but your bombs won't be doing much from inside my pocket."

The Rhino's face turned to stone. He had a look of utter confusion. He didn't know whether to laugh or feel terrified. He snorted loudly then spat a ball of mucus onto the floor.

"What are you talking about?" he asked nervously. "There's no way you could have gotten all those bombs. You're bluffing."

Micro Dad didn't answer. He reached into his utility belt and fumbled around inside before pulling out the small glass bottle that contained the bombs. He shook the bottle, causing the explosives to sway like flakes in a snow globe.

The Rhino squinted. They were too small for him to see with his small button-like eyes, but he knew it was true. His finger slid away from the trigger, then he placed the detonator back into his pocket. His mouth tightened to keep from yelling in a fit of rage. He had failed. There was no way he could destroy Alex's lungs.

"No more tricks, Rhino. It's just you and me now, and you have nothing left to threaten me with."

The virus was close to exploding. His jaw locked tight, and his eyes darkened. He stood motionless and stared at Micro Dad. The hero had ruined everything and would have to pay for it.

The Rhino's chest rose and fell quickly as he breathed. Then without warning, the virus lifted his weapon and tapped the trigger twice. Two shots erupted out of the rusty, old weapon. One raced toward the top of Micro Dad's helmet, while the other moved toward the center of his chest.

Micro Dad didn't flinch. He stood like a matador and waited for the perfect moment to dodge the two beams of light. When they reached him, he slid his hand to his wrist and pressed a button. In the blink of an eye, he vanished, and the two shots flew past the shadow where his body once stood.

He reappeared in a flash, standing in the same spot. The Rhino released another round of shots. Micro Dad quickly evaded them. He smiled then disappeared once again before he could be hit.

The Rhino held his weapon out in front of him while he searched the area around him again and again, waiting for Micro Dad to pop up like a game of *Whac-A-Mole*, but seconds ticked by without him returning. So cautiously, the virus slowly walked down the aisle. He crept along silently and waited for Micro Dad to show himself.

He scanned every item that was close to him but found nothing. Suddenly, a bright light appeared in a seat behind him. The Rhino spun around to aim his weapon, but before he could, Micro Dad's foot moved across the seat and into the aisle then kicked the weapon out of his hands. It sailed into the air before falling and sliding down the aisle. It stopped once it slid underneath a row of seats.

The Rhino watched it as it came to a stop. He quickly turned back to see Micro Dad pointing the micro-gun at him. His mind raced.

The only thing he could think to say was, "Let's make a deal. You were willing to let me go before, right?"

A moment later, a shot rang out.

Chapter 30

A shot of zinc hurtled toward The Rhino, but with tremendous speed, the virus swung his head and hit the ball as if it were a pitch. It connected with a loud thwack and sent the shot crashing into the wall at the back of the plane where it splattered on impact. Shocked, Micro Dad fired again. This time, The Rhino hit the zinc back at Micro Dad, who quickly vanished before getting struck.

When he reappeared, The Rhino was directly in front of him. The virus sprang forward, lunging at him. His dagger-like horn flew at Micro Dad, but as the horn rose to meet him, Micro Dad held out his weapon to catch the blow.

The horn slammed into the micro-gun. The ivory-colored spike was dangerously sharp but still not enough to pierce through the micro-gun. The crash only left a small dent in its metal frame, but the blow was powerful enough to knock Micro Dad backward into the wall of the plane.

The Rhino took a step back then lunged again. He grunted like a bull as he shifted all his weight toward Micro Dad, but instead of ramming the weapon, the tip of the Rhino's horn gently fell into the small gap near its trigger. It fit like a lock and key. Micro Dad tried to pull his weapon free, but The Rhino yanked his head back defiantly like a dog fighting over a chew toy. He pulled his head up and back with a hard jerk, yanking the gun from Micro Dad's hands, then he tossed it into a seat behind him.

The Rhino's mouth immediately curled into a smile as he

hissed, "Looks like I'm the only one with a weapon."

He charged forward wildly for what he assumed would be the last time, but before his horn could reach the armored suit, Micro Dad vanished.

The virus nearly speared the plane's wall as he dove through a single puff of light. He jumped back and searched the seats around him. His small eyes lowered even more as he squinted to catch a glimpse of Micro Dad.

"Stop running and fight!" The Rhino shouted but received only silence in return.

Suddenly, a tiny flash zipped across his face. It was there one moment then gone the next. The Rhino's eyes moved like the hands of a clock to find it. They went up then down, finally stopping when they reached his horn.

He saw a tiny speck in the middle of it. His eyes crossed, but he could barely see. He wasn't staring long before he realized the speck was moving towards him, doubling in size along the way. It grew from a dot to a miniature Micro Dad in seconds. The toy-like figure raced down the Rhino's horn then leaped into the air. His legs stretched out and the bottoms of his boots were spread wide.

The Rhino's hands shot up to protect himself, but he was too late. Micro Dad's boots rammed into his face right on top of his eyebrow. Micro Dad was about the size of the Rhino's horn, but the kick landed with a deafening crack that sent the virus falling backwards into the seats behind him.

Micro Dad crashed to the floor then quickly stood up and returned to the size of The Rhino. He took a few steps forward and found the wide-bodied virus toppled over the entire row, completely still. Micro Dad cautiously stood over him to look for signs that he was still alive but couldn't find any. The Rhino's large chest was motionless.

Micro Dad inched closer. The Rhino's eyes were shut, so he was sure the virus was lifeless. His eyes studied The Rhino's face. His rough grey skin looked as strong and as thick as leather. Scars from countless invasions were scattered across it. Micro Dad began to wonder how he had gotten them all in his pursuit of destroying humans. A small part of him even began to feel sympathy for him as he took his eyes off the virus.

In a flash, The Rhino's eyes shot open. They were dark but full of rage. Micro Dad took a step back to escape, but The Rhino was faster. He pulled his legs back to his round belly then kicked out.

His feet collided with Micro Dad's midsection, knocking him to his knees. He almost collapsed on the floor but caught himself and remained on all fours while he gasped for breath. His eyes looked onto the ground below him as he fought to take in air. He was completely unaware The Rhino was already on his feet and standing over him. A wide grin spread across his face, showing every one of his stained teeth. He snorted then spat clear across Micro Dad's helmet and onto the floor.

"Are you okay, Micro Dad?" he asked sarcastically. "You don't look so good. Let me help you up," he bellowed then lifted his foot and brought it crashing down on top of Micro Dad's back. He immediately fell flat on the ground.

"Sorry about that," he laughed, "I'm a little clumsy sometimes. I'll give you a hand." He balled one hand into a fist that looked more like a sledgehammer then swung it at the back of Micro Dad's helmet. He missed but caught him in the left shoulder. The blow was powerful enough to knock him deeper into the floor.

Micro Dad groaned. He heard bells ringing in his ears, and he was dizzy. He planted his hands into the floor and tried to push himself up, but his arms shook as if they were made of jelly. He tried his best to lift himself, but he quickly failed. His arms were too weak, so he fell back to the floor.

The Rhino roared with laughter. He snorted and wheezed. He bent over as he cackled. It took him a moment to stand upright, which Micro Dad was thankful for, as he wouldn't suffer any more pain, but it was short-lived. The virus stopped laughing soon after, but a smirk still hung from his lips.

He couldn't let the chance to torment Micro Dad slip away. "The infamous Micro Dad. I've heard so many stories about you and all the germs you've defeated. Is this it?" he asked, wagging a finger. "I'm disappointed."

He sank low to the ground then pressed both hands firmly against the cold metal floor. Next, he dropped his head as if he were a grazing cow. It hung next to Micro Dad's limp body. He grunted loudly, then with a tremendous burst of speed and power, he thrust his horn up and out to land another blow.

It struck Micro Dad in the center of his chest, right in the middle of the stethoscope and thermometer emblem that lay there. Somehow, the sharp horn still couldn't pierce his armor, but it lifted him off the ground easily. He soared through the air, spinning as he went up for what felt like hours. His eyes opened during the flight, and all he could see was The Rhino's face with a beaming smile.

The rollercoaster finally ended when he crashed into the ceiling. His belly hit first. He spread his arms out wide in an attempt to grab ahold of anything within sight, but the roof was too smooth. His fingers slid off, and he soon plummeted down to the floor and landed with a hard clunk.

His thin, form-fitting armor still gleamed brightly and barely had a scratch on it. Luckily for him, the suit was designed to absorb powerful attacks, but it was beginning to lose some of its strength. Micro Dad could feel every bit of the punishment he had endured. His muscles ached even more.

He was in pain and could hardly move, but quitting wasn't an option for him. He lifted his head and scanned the area around him. Immediately, he recognized that he had fallen near the back of the plane. He had somehow been thrown from one end of it to the other. He looked over his shoulder and saw The Rhino slowly making his way down the aisle, whistling as he strolled. Micro Dad knew he had a little more time.

He peered over his shoulder again to see The Rhino inching toward him. With his energy nearly all gone, Micro Dad slowly reached into a pocket of his utility belt. He fought to stand. His body groaned with every shaky movement, but he managed to get to his feet. It took him a second to find his balance without collapsing, but he managed that too after a moment.

His hand curled into a fist as he slid it out of his pocket and placed it at his side just as The Rhino approached him, still whistling a happy tune. They were back within steps of each other. The Rhino stood strong and defiant while Micro Dad looked as if he could crumble at any moment.

The Rhino hit a final high note to end the song. He continued to smile cheerfully as he stared at Micro Dad. "You got guts, Micro Dad. I'll give you that," he said. "Not a lot of white cells could take those hits from my horn and keep standing, but I guess you're not a weak white cell," he chuckled. "The white cells are no match for me, and neither are you."

Micro Dad didn't move or speak.

The Rhino shifted his head from left to right, cracking his neck loudly. "I think one more hit oughtta do it."

He prepared to charge. He stomped his feet against the floor one-by-one as if he were building up speed.

Micro Dad stood motionless. He didn't have much fight left. His entire body still felt weak, but he had a plan. He kept both feet rooted in place, and he waited.

The ground rumbled as The Rhino continued to stomp tirelessly. The sound was like a heavy bass drum. Suddenly, the virus sprinted forward. He moved like an Olympic sprinter and closed the distance between them in seconds. He lowered his horn, ready to deliver the final blow.

Time slowed. Even with The Rhino racing toward him, Micro Dad didn't move a muscle. He waited for the horn to get closer. His hand opened slightly, revealing a small disk in his palm.

Just as the tip of the horn was about to spear him, Micro Dad dove to his right. His hand opened wider. Then with a gentle toss, the disk sailed through the space between him and the virus. In an instant, it stuck to the bottom of The Rhino's horn.

The Rhino's speed forced him forward. He almost collided with the back wall of the plane but managed to catch himself before puncturing it. His arms hit the wall with enough force that the entire aircraft shook wildly. Anger quickly boiled inside him.

He quickly turned to find Micro Dad lifting himself off the ground. The Rhino grunted noisily then planted his feet to launch another attack. He stomped them hard against the metal floor and prepared to sprint forward once again. But before he had time to move, Micro Dad shouted, "Time's up, Rhino. You infected the wrong person."

The Rhino had a look of disbelief wrapped in terror. He stood frozen in place with his mouth hanging open as he watched Micro Dad's hand travel to his wrist and press a button. A sudden flash of light erupted and filled the plane. Seconds later, the light was gone, and so was The Rhino.

Chapter 31

The Rhino vanished in the blink of an eye, but he wasn't gone completely. Micro Dad pulled a small empty bottle out of his pocket. He removed its lid then held the bottle on its side as he bent down and searched the floor in front of him. Then in one motion, he used the tip of his finger to scoop a tiny dot into it.

He lifted the glass bottle to his eyes and stared into it. It was difficult to see, but he could just make out The Rhino standing at the bottom of it. The virus pounded the glass and used his horn to scratch the walls, but he was too small to cause any damage. The bottle didn't move.

Micro Dad continued to watch The Rhino for a second longer. The tiny speck seemed to hurl insults at him, but his voice was too weak for Micro Dad to hear. So, he put the lid on the bottle then placed it gently back into his utility belt. He breathed a sigh of relief but only for a moment. He realized the plane was still in autopilot.

He raced to the cockpit and pressed the button to disengage the plane's self-flying mechanism. He gripped the controls, then he immediately turned the plane around to fly it back to Phil and the other white cells. It took time, but he eventually found the right alleyway due to the cluster of white cells that still stood on the rooftops of the nearby factories. He landed quickly and darted out of the plane.

To his surprise, the white cells all began cheering at the sight of him. Even Chief T, who stood at the top of a building, had a soft smile. They all applauded and patted him on the back as Micro Dad limped through the large crowd to find Phil. When he finally found the cell, Phil was giving high-fives to members of his team but abruptly stopped when he saw Micro Dad. He quickly rushed to him.

"You don't look so good," he said playfully.

"I feel even worse," Micro Dad answered back with a smile. "How's the rookie?"

"He's going to make it. We had him taken back to HQ. He's getting treatment for his wounds."

"That's great to hear. I would have hated to lose another cell to The Rhino."

"Me too," said Phil, becoming tense. "Where is the little germ, anyway?"

Micro Dad patted his utility belt. "In here for safe keeping. Then he's getting locked up in my lab for good."

"Make sure he's locked up tight. He can be tricky."

"Don't worry," said Micro Dad, "my lab is one of the most well-guarded places on Earth. I have dozens of germs locked up in there."

Phil nodded then took a few moments to speak. "Thanks for all your help, Micro Dad. It was great working with you."

He held out a hand, which Micro Dad accepted. "You're the real hero, PJ. It was great working with you, too."

"Wish Alex luck in the science fair for me," Phil added.

"I will," said Micro Dad, taking out the micro-plane.

They finished shaking hands then Micro Dad ran through the crowd of cells. Once he was in the open, he threw the plane into the air and watched it instantly float. He turned back to look at the cells for a final time then pressed a button on his wrist. In a flash, he was gone.

Soon after, the micro-plane lifted higher into the air. It grew larger the higher it rose. It elevated above the factory for a moment longer then rocketed off, racing toward the lung's exit.

Chapter 32

Alex woke up in a daze. He didn't realize he had fallen asleep. Part of him thought that it was still morning and that he had woken up for the first time. He hoped the entire day had been a dream, but when he looked down and saw that he was still wearing the mismatched clothes and had the walkie-talkie tucked under his arm, he knew it was real. He really had been sick, and he really couldn't go to the science fair. His dad really was a microscopic superhero who had shrunk to an incredibly small size just to fight the cold virus that had made him sick.

He sat up and climbed down off the bed. He was still a little tired, but it steadily faded, then he realized he felt great. There was no more runny nose, sore throat, and harsh cough. Even the lymph node underneath his chin felt better. He smiled and inhaled deeply, enjoying the ease of breathing, then he glanced down at his cellphone and almost screamed when he saw the time.

He only had thirty minutes left to make it to the science fair. He opened his phone and found more messages from Josh and Aiden, asking where he was and if he could bring a bag of chips. That was from Aiden. There were also a few missed calls. Those were from his mom, so he ignored them.

"Oh, man!" He exclaimed. "I'm gonna miss it. Dad, where are you?"

He sighed, suddenly feeling a tickle in his nose. It felt as if dust had floated into it. Alex quickly began to sniffle and wiggle his nose from side to side. It was all he could do to fight back a sneeze.

He started with an "A-A-A" and before he could finish the "C-C-C-HOOOO", a flash of light exploded in the center of the room. It lasted for less than a second then disappeared, leaving behind Micro Dad.

A huge grin showed through his helmet. He pressed a button on his wrist, then the mask instantly vanished. He immediately ran to Alex, who had an even bigger smile spread across his face.

"How you feelin', Al?" he asked while running a hand over the top of his son's head playfully.

"Dad, you're back!" Alex shouted. "That was amazing. Can you show me how you do that? Can I try on the suit? What happened? Was The Rhino ugly? Oh, and I feel great."

Micro Dad chuckled lightly. "I'm glad you're okay, Al. I'll tell you all about it."

For several minutes, Micro Dad told Alex about the entire mission while Alex sat in silence and listened, too stunned to talk. Terror washed over him when Micro Dad got to the part about The Rhino using a vortex to destroy the white cell's headquarters and Alex's lymph nodes. He became angry when he heard about the rookie getting injured. But ultimately, he was relieved that Micro Dad had won. Then for the finale, Micro Dad pulled the tiny bottle from his utility belt and held it out in front of him so Alex could see.

"It was tough, but I finally got him," he said, pointing at the clear bottle.

Alex looked confused. He was waiting to see a scary virus but saw nothing but empty space.

"Where is he? Did he escape already?" Alex asked suspiciously.

"No, Al. I could see him after I captured him, but he's too

small to see out here. He's in there, and trust me, he's mad."

"That's incredible. Thanks, Dad."

Micro Dad flashed a warm smile. "We better get going. We don't want to miss the science fair, right?" Then he looked Alex up and down. "Is this what you're wearing? I like it."

"You really think we can make it?" Alex asked excitedly. "We have less than twenty-five minutes to get there."

"Then we better hurry up and change," Micro Dad said as he quickly turned and hurried out of the door.

Chapter 33

Alex sprinted as if he were in a race. He changed into a faded pair of jeans and a t-shirt then stuffed his remote-controlled car into his bookbag and ran down the hall to Frank's office. He found his dad already dressed in his usual khaki pants and collar shirt. They hurried down the stairs together and were out of the door in seconds.

Once they were in the car, Alex turned to Frank and asked, "Why don't we take the micro-plane. Isn't it way faster?"

"No way, Alex," Frank said, starting the ignition. "I don't use the micro-plane for everyday stuff. It's for germ-fighting use only."

Alex just shrugged. "Ah, man. I wanted to see it."

"You will someday," Frank said as he backed the car out of the driveway.

The school was normally less than five minutes away, but traffic and school buses added an extra ten to their drive. Alex's leg shook impatiently while he stared at the clock in the center of the car's dashboard. Every passing minute made him more nervous. Frank sensed his son's anxiety, so he played some music to ease his mind. After a few minutes, Alex began to relax, and they spent the rest of the car ride rapping along to hip hop songs.

They made it with only three minutes left to spare. It was a rule that every contestant had to be inside of the school's gym by three thirty or they would be prevented from competing. Frank quickly parked the car in the first open spot he could find. They jumped out and ran toward the large building.

A group of people were being ushered through a pair of double doors one at time. The last of them entered while Frank and Alex were still crossing the parking lot. They were only a few feet away when the doors began to close. They called out for the doorman to stop as they ran, but luckily, they managed to rush inside just before the doors slammed shut.

Immediately, they were hit by the sound of loud chattering and a variety of weird sounds coming from the other kids, who were showing onlookers whatever gadget they had created. Alex walked ahead of Frank and stared at the rows of booths that went in five lines across the gym. More than thirty kids were competing, and Alex could see they had interesting inventions just like his. Electronic motors sputtered. There were aquariums and terrariums filled with all kinds of animals that had been studied and written about.

Alex gawked at them all until he suddenly heard his name being yelled above dozens of conversations. The voice was familiar. It had a hint of anger that was enough to make both Alex and Frank shudder. They turned in surprise.

Camille stormed through a group of people who were admiring a student's hissing cockroach farm. She grimaced as she walked past it. When she finally reached Frank and Alex, she stopped and stared at them for a moment. She had perfected a look over the years of which Frank and Alex could never tell how mad she was. The look was intense and always made them confess to whatever it was she wanted them to. She didn't have to use it often, but it worked every time whenever she did.

Frank and Alex were worried that "the look" was coming. Alex wasn't sure he would be able to hold in the details of Micro Dad's adventure. Fortunately for him, after a few seconds, her eyes softened, and her mouth curled into a smile.

"I knew you two would be here," she said as she stepped closer and shoved them both. "Is that why you weren't answering my calls? Because you wanted to sneak here without me knowing?"

Frank hesitated for a moment before he could speak. "Uh, yeah. Of course. We should've known better than to try and fool your mom," Frank said while giving Alex a wink then leaned forward to take her in his arms.

"That's right," she said, pushing him away playfully then turning to Alex, "but you shouldn't be here if you're sick, baby. Your dad should know better."

Alex immediately cringed. He quickly looked around, making sure no one had heard the embarrassing nickname. Once he was sure no one had, he turned back to her and rolled his eyes.

"Don't call me that, Mom. That's embarrassing."

"You'll always be my baby, baby. But don't change the subject. Why are you here when you're sick? Frank, you're a doctor, right? Can you explain this?"

"Dad, uh, Dad helped me get better," Alex said quickly, turning to Frank. "I mean, he didn't help me get better. It's not like he beat up germs or anything. I mean, that would be ridiculous. Because that's not possible. I mean, uh, Dad gave me soup and medicine and stuff, and now I feel better. That's all. Right, Dad?"

Camille turned to Frank with a confused look on her face. He was just nodding his head in agreement. "Okay," she said. Her look was changing from confused to outright suspicious. "You really feel better already?"

"He's fine. Right, Al?" Frank said quickly.

"Fine," Alex replied and gave a thumbs up.

Suddenly, Alex heard his name once again. He turned to see Josh and Aiden running towards him. Aiden reached him first. They greeted each other with the secret handshake the trio had made up years before. Their hands collided then intertwined in a series of well-rehearsed movements. It was complicated to anyone who watched them, but they had perfected it and made it look easy.

"Where've you been, bro? We thought you weren't gonna show up," said Aiden.

He was beaming like always, ready for Alex to slip up and say anything he could use to turn into a joke. His wide grin sat high up on his slender face, underneath a pair of dark, deep-set eyes. He was taller than the other two by a little more than two inches but seemed to tower over them because his large afro gave the illusion that he was much taller. This all sat atop a slim, wiry frame and came equipped with long, tentacle-like arms.

Before Alex could respond, Josh stepped in front of Aiden and spoke. "You're lucky you made it on time. What happened?" he said with his typical twelve-going-on-forty tone.

He was the total opposite of Aiden. He had a calm, grown-up attitude. His face was round and kind. He had thoughtful eyes that were partially hidden behind a pair of wide-framed glasses. He was shorter and more heavyset, but he moved like a cat, especially when he played soccer. He had been the best player in school every year since second grade and was captain of their team, a fact he never let Alex and Aiden forget.

"It's a long story," Alex said quickly, thinking about his earlier missteps with his mom, "but I'm here now, and nothing's beating this." He held up his bookbag. "I need to find my booth and set up my display."

Aiden found his opening. "We already know where it is," he

announced with a sly smile.

Alex recognized the look and knew immediately that it couldn't be good. He was worried but forced himself to ask the question. "Where is it?"

Aiden and Josh pointed in unison, and both wore huge grins across their faces. Alex let his parents know he was going to set up his booth and would see them later, then he slowly followed his friends to find it. They squeezed through dozens of people on their way until they reached three booths located in the middle of the gym. The one to their left was occupied by a sixth grader named Elyse Douglass, who had made a diorama about the importance of bees. She was quiet and barely ever spoke in class except when the topic was about preserving nature.

Alex's booth was in the middle, but he didn't care. He only wanted to see his other neighbor. The two walls that enclosed it were a cold grey, making the box seem dull. They made it through a surprisingly large crowd that had already formed to admire the bright blues and greens that exploded out of real pictures of the Earth taken from outer space. They were amazing and looked as if someone had done a photoshoot on the outer edge of the planet.

Alex looked down at the table and saw a folded sign that read "How to Save the Planet". Behind that was a box. It was chrome on two sides and clear on the top and middle, which provided a view of a series of wheels and other equipment that never stopped turning.

Suddenly, a lid opened. Alex watched as someone placed a plastic water bottle inside. The wheels and machinery began to spin faster, moving the bottle from one end to the other as if it were a factory assembly line. The process lasted less than a minute, and once the bottle reached the other side, the machine spit out what was left.

Alex couldn't believe it, but the bottle was transformed into a marble-sized globe with all seven continents clearly defined. Alex stared, amazed. It was so well done. He looked closer and saw the initials ZP etched into the marble's center. Alex's heart began to race, and his palms began to sweat.

He had seen the initials over a million times. They were on high scorer lists, artwork, and even between pages of textbooks throughout the years. So, he knew exactly who they belonged to. His suspicions were confirmed a second later when Zoey Perez began to speak.

"So, you see, ladies and gentlemen," she said as clear and well-spoken as ever, "my machine turns plastic into tiny works of art that can be collected or even worn as jewelry."

She stepped to the center of the table and flashed a pair of earrings with tiny globes dangling from them. She was all smiles as she presented them, showing each of the blue and green rubber bands that lined the braces on her teeth as she turned from left to right. Her long, curly hair flowed down over her t-shirt, which was another picture of the Earth with "How to Save the Planet" written across the front.

After a few seconds, she continued, "I found dozens of plastic bottles at the park. I volunteer there on weekends to make sure it stays clean. So you can all have your very first one. You can all help us save this wonderful planet we call home."

The crowd applauded loudly. Zoey kept her smile then added a wave. She was acting as if she had already won. She looked out into the crowd and began mouthing "Thank you" to each person.

To Alex's relief, the applause finally ended, and the crowd began to fade away to see other projects.

When they were all gone, Zoey turned to Alex and shouted,

"Look who decided to get some guts and show up, Alexander the Loser. You like my invention?" she asked mockingly. "I've been working on it for over a year. My dad helped me design it. He's an astronaut, you know. That's how I got the cool pictures."

Alex, along with the entire sixth grade, knew that Zoey's dad was an astronaut. She mentioned it almost daily. She even said he would be on the first mission to Mars and would bring her back some Martian rocks. It made Alex sick.

"Whatever, Zoey. Your invention is, uh, okay," he said casually, "but it's got nothin' on this." He reached into his bookbag and pulled out his car so Zoey could get a good look at it.

"That's right. You goin' down today, Zoey," Aiden interjected from behind Alex's shoulder.

Zoey's face turned red. Her smile widened, then she began to laugh hysterically. It took her over a minute to recover. When she finally did, she pointed at the car and giggled.

"You really think you can beat me with that thing? Congrats, you found an old, beat-up toy car in a dumpster somewhere." She couldn't help but roar with laughter once again.

Alex scowled then marched over to his booth. He could still hear her laughing as he placed his car and bookbag on the table. He reached inside the bag and removed the key element to his invention. It was a normal plastic bag filled with wet brown dirt. He threw it on the table, and it landed with a hard thud.

Josh and Aiden glanced at each other. Josh had a look of concern while Aiden had a look of curiosity.

"What's with the dirt, man?" Josh asked as Alex opened the bag, releasing the smell of fresh earth.

"This is the energy source for my car," he said loudly as if his question were silly.

Aiden chuckled. "This is dirt, Alex. You need a battery, gas, trash, or somethin'."

Alex didn't look up from his work. He picked up his car then pressed a small button underneath it to open its hood as if he were changing the oil. He dug into his bag again and took out a tiny spoon he used to scoop piles of dirt into a circular hole where the engine would be. When the dirt was packed into it well enough, Alex started to shut the lid, but before he did, he pointed to two small wires that hung from the hood.

"You see these wires?" he asked. "These wires are copper and go down into the dirt, like this." Alex slowly lowered the hood, watching the two wires slowly fall into the dirt until they disappeared.

"Different types of bacteria and other microbes live in soil," he continued, "probably billions. When the microbes eat nutrients in the dirt, they give off some energy. I built the car to run off that energy."

He placed the car on the far side of the table then picked up the remote that hung out of his bookbag.

"The same for the remote. Nothing but dirt," he added.

He turned it on and gripped the remote with both hands as he pointed it at the toy car. His fingers fell on top of the two joysticks that sat in the middle of the remote. With a flick of his thumbs, he moved the joysticks forward. In response, the car's tires screeched, then it raced forward and reached the other side of the table in no time at all.

Josh and Aiden erupted. "That's awwwsooomme."

Alex smiled brightly as he moved the sticks from left to right then up and down. Each time the car moved. It made a figure-eight then made doughnuts in the table's plastic. It traveled back and forth across the table dozens of times.

Aiden continued to shout so loud that a crowd began to form around Alex's booth. It started with only a few people at first but soon swelled to a huge number. Josh and Aiden were sure to tell everyone that the car was dirt-powered then explained how it worked. The crowd listened and huddled closely together to watch Alex drive the car back and forth while Aiden took breaks to say, "It's running on dirt, people. Dirt."

Frank and Camille also heard the commotion and joined the growing crowd. Almost everyone in the gym made their way over to see Alex drive the car. Even Zoey had to take a peek out of her booth to see. Her face was fixed into a scowl the entire time while watching Alex's performance.

Alex absorbed every bit of the spotlight. He flipped the switches and made the car do even more tricks. He even managed to do a wheelie with the car driving on its two left wheels. The crowd erupted into applause yet again.

Eventually, the dirt in the car dried out, and the car started losing power. Alex rushed to empty the old dirt into a coffee cup he kept in his bookbag then refilled the container with fresh wet dirt to continue driving.

Moments later, three wide-eyed people squeezed through the crowd and stood between Alex and Zoey's booths. Each one wore a red ribbon with "Judge" printed on it. They all carried a clipboard with a list of every science fair participant, and each one held a different trophy ranging from first to third.

One of them, a tall, heavyset woman, who stood in the middle of the three, waved one of her hands to silence the crowd then glared at Aiden to silence him. The entire gym fell silent. Her name was Vice Principal Cruz. She had taught at Lincoln Middle School for almost eleven years and was always known for joking with students as they walked the halls.

Her belly hung over her waist. Long, wild hair flowed all the way down to the middle of her back. She had laugh lines throughout her face from her constant smiling, but it made the kids love her. After a moment, she opened her mouth to speak, and her strong voice filled the room.

"This has probably been one of the best science fairs that I've ever attended. You kids all did a fantastic job. You sure you guys are only in the sixth grade?" she asked, getting a few light laughs from the crowd before continuing. "There are no losers here today, but we do have to give trophies to the three individuals we thought did the best. We've seen every invention here today, and we've come to a decision."

Whispers followed, but she continued, "I'll read the names of the students who have won first, second and third place. This was a really difficult decision. You all did so well."

Cheers washed over the entire crowd. Alex's heart immediately started to race. He was unbelievably nervous. He didn't know what to do with his hands. He set them flat on the table then folded them across his chest before finally putting them into his pockets.

Vice Principal Cruz cleared her throat, then the room fell completely silent. "Third place goes to—" There was a dramatic pause for added effect. "Zoey Perez with her How to Save the Planet machine."

The crowd clapped loudly. Alex's heart almost leapt from his chest. He forced a smile then brought his hands together and clapped with the rest of the crowd. He looked over at Zoey, who was accepting her trophy. An awkward grin fell across her face as she thanked the judges.

She continued, "Congratulations, Zoey. Second place goes to—"

The room fell silent again, and the silence seemed to last for hours. Alex tried hard to hold in his excitement and nerves, but he was ready to explode. He watched as Vice Principal Cruz held out the trophy and read the name off the clipboard.

"Alex Freeman."

For a moment, Alex was frozen in time. He heard his name called, but for some reason, his brain wouldn't work. A blank look sat on his face. The crowd erupted into applause. He could hear his parents' shouts above the rest.

He stared out to find them, but they were lost in a sea of students, teachers, and other parents. It wasn't until the judge called his name again then walked over to him with the trophy that Alex began to thaw. His hands trembled as he held them out and accepted the trophy. It was in the shape of a microscope and had "Science Fair 2nd Place" engraved into its silver finish. The award gleamed from the bright lights in the gym. He traced the "2nd Place" with his fingers, not knowing how to feel.

Soon after, Vice Principal Cruz announced first place. It went to Jaylen Andrews, a shy kid whom Alex didn't know very well even though he was in almost all of Alex's classes. The crowd and judges loved his robotic puppy. They couldn't get enough of how realistic it was, even down to its shrill, puppy-like bark.

Jaylen received his trophy, then all three students lined up together for pictures. Zoey and Alex stood beside each other without saying a word. When enough pictures had been taken, Alex shook hands with Jaylen to congratulate him. He turned to Zoey afterwards, but she was already halfway to the gym door with her parents. Before walking out, she turned and gave Alex a light smile then was gone.

The crowd quickly disappeared as well. Alex was left alone

with his trophy for only a moment. His parents and friends approached him. They all had great, huge smiles. Josh and Aiden gave him high-fives and told him how cool his invention was, Aiden adding that he should have won.

Frank and Camille hugged him and said how proud they were of him.

"Let's go celebrate. Who wants pizza?" Camille asked, quickly getting a response from Aiden and Josh.

"What about Maya?" asked Frank.

"We'll pick her up on the way. Let's go."

The crowd continued to leave the gym, so they all followed. Camille, Josh, and Aiden led the way. They made their way to the double doors leading outside. Alex walked beside Frank quietly. Frank noticed and glanced down at him.

"You okay, Al? I know how much you wanted to win, but your car really is amazing," he said with a smile.

Alex didn't respond right away. He looked down at his trophy then started to smile. "Today has been such a weird day," he said. "I actually talked to one of my own white blood cells today. How crazy is that? But the coolest part about today was finding out you were Micro Dad."

Frank beamed, thinking about his mission, Chief T, Phil, and the other cells.

"I may not have won first place," Alex continued, "but it's been a pretty good day. Besides, did you see the look on Zoey's face when she saw me win second? It was priceless."

The two howled with laughter. Frank placed an arm around Alex's shoulders, and they walked out of the gym and into the cool autumn air.

Epilogue

Alex quietly crept into Frank's office to find him moving throughout the small space that sat hidden behind the bookshelf. It was well lit. Bright light from two powerful LED bulbs flooded the space, making the microscopes and other laboratory equipment easy to see.

Frank held a glass bottle marked as "The Rhinovirus" then walked up to a large square box. He entered a four-digit code that released its sliding door, freeing a cloud of ice-cold smoke. He carefully placed the bottle inside it before reentering the code again and closing the door. Then he turned and saw Alex and nearly jumped.

"You can't just go around sneaking up on people, Al," he said with a laugh. "You know, you're the only other person who knows about this place. I keep a lot of bad germs locked up here in this machine. It freezes the viruses and bacteria instantly but makes sure they stay alive. I like to think of it like a super-cold prison for germs." He laughed again, then his expression grew serious. "I can trust you to keep this place a secret, right?"

Alex smiled brightly. "I'm your sidekick, remember? I wanna help."

A grin flashed across Frank's face. He just stared at Alex without speaking. At that moment, he knew his adventures as Micro Dad were just beginning.

"You're not my sidekick, Al. You're my partner."

He left the hollowed-out space then pressed a button on the

side of the bookshelf in front of him, triggering the shelf to close, covering every inch of the secret lab. Frank followed Alex out of the office then flipped a switch to turn out the light.

Alex turned toward his room while Frank stood outside of his office, but before they parted ways, the two looked at each other for a final time that night. They were both exhausted from the day's events. They didn't speak. Their eyes did the talking for them, acknowledging that they shared an even stronger bond. Then after a moment, they turned away and continued on to their rooms, finding their beds and settling in for some much-needed rest.